Need You Now

by

J. Kenner

Need You Now Copyright © 2018 by Julie Kenner

Cover design by Covers by Rogenna

Cover image by Perrywinkle Photography

ISBN: 978-1-940673-73-8

Published by Martini & Olive Books

v. 2018_2_8_P

Chapter One

"YOU, my friend, have got some big, sparkly balls."

Cameron Reed took a long, satisfied swallow of beer as he stared at the finger pointing straight at his face. He was seated at a four-top near the front window of The Fix on Sixth, a popular Austin bar where he worked as a bartender when he wasn't at the University or, like today, enjoying a day off.

The finger in question belonged to Nolan Wood, a local radio personality and frequent customer at The Fix.

Darryl Silver sat in the only other occupied chair. Cam's best friend since before puberty, Darryl had just arrived back in town after graduating from law school. "Someone going to tell me why we're praising my buddy's *cojones*?" Darryl asked.

"Duh," Cam said scooting his chair back and cupping his package. "Because they are worthy of some serious praise, didn't you know?"

Darryl snorted, then turned to look at Nolan. "How about *you* tell me? Our boy's ego's getting in the way of my edification."

"There he goes again, talking like a baby lawyer," Cam quipped as Darryl shot him the finger.

Nolan ignored the jibes, his attention on Darryl. "Because even though Cam didn't win the contest for Mr. February, he and his *cojones* definitely made a splash."

Cam grabbed a Loaded Hush Puppy out of a paper-lined plastic basket and popped it in his mouth. It might be Cam's day off, but The Fix was as much a home as his room near campus or the tiny South Austin house where he and his sister had grown up, and he'd come here to hang out, have lunch, and enjoy life in front of the bar.

A few tables over, Tiffany, one of the waitresses caught his eye. He lifted his beer to signal for another, and she gave him a nod in acknowledgment as she delivered drinks and burgers. Even though the crowds were the biggest at night, The Fix had a steady lunchtime clientele.

Cam leaned back again, mimicking Nolan's relaxed posture. "You know," he said, "I don't think I made a splash. More like a statement."

"Ha!" Nolan practically barked the word. "That's the truth. *Comic relief,*" he said, shaking his head as if reliving a happy memory. "I mean, you gotta love it."

"Maybe *you* do," Darryl said, putting down his rum and Coke. "But I don't know what the hell you're talking about. Comic relief? Mr. February? What does—Oh, wait." He turned to Cameron. "This has something to do with that Calendar Guy contest, doesn't it? Mina told me a little about that."

At the mention of Darryl's twin sister, Cam felt the familiar tightening in his gut, as well as parts further south. He'd had a crush on Mina Silver for half his life, and he'd known her longer than that. She was his best friend's twin sister, after all, so she'd been a constant presence. The girl they teased, the pest they shooed away.

Or she had been, until Cam had begun to notice her sweet smile, her quirky sense of humor. Until he realized that half the time when he went to Darryl's house during summer break, his motive was less about playing video games with his buddy and more about catching a glimpse of Mina.

And then one day, he'd seen her at the mall making out with Tony Renfroe, a high school quarterback whose picture was all over the local paper.

That's when the monster had stirred inside Cameron. A wild, craving beast that had wanted to lash out and knock Tony right off his pedestal—and out of Mina's arms.

Except he hadn't given in to that monster. Not then. Not later.

And Mina had dated Tony. Then Alex. Then Roger. And God only knew who else.

Never Cam, though. And over the years his crush had ramped up, escalating past the warm, gooey thoughts he'd had as a teenager to the current line-up of full-color, X-rated dreams that had him waking up twined in his sheets with the kind of painful boner that even a cold shower couldn't tame.

"Yeah," Nolan said, in response to Darryl's question. "The Mr. February contest was this past Wednesday. I gotta say, The Fix has only had two contests so far, but I'm already hearing a lot of buzz around town. I think they really have something here."

Darryl opened his mouth, apparently to point out that he still wasn't entirely up to speed, but Cam jumped in first, explaining about the contest and the other changes being implemented at The Fix, all designed to up the bar's revenue.

As a bartender, Cam only knew the high points that Tyree, the bar's owner, had told him. The bottom line being that The Fix had run into some financial trouble —mostly because of competing corporate chain bars that had moved in, offering discounted drinks and scantily clad waitresses.

The bottom line? If the bar's revenue didn't increase significantly by the end of the calendar year, then The Fix would have to close its doors.

That situation had been spelled out to Cam and the other employees at a staff meeting, along with the fact that Tyree had partnered with Reece Walker, Brent Sinclair, and Jenna Montgomery to make it happen.

Reece, the bar's manager, had been Cam's immediate boss since he'd signed on. A former cop, Brent was in charge of all the security. Jenna hadn't been an employee before coming on board, but she had a marketing background and had implemented a whole slew of changes and promotions designed to increase revenue, the customer base, and the bar's overall reputation around town.

From Cam's perspective, the biggest coup for the bar was the fact that it was home base for *The Business Plan*, a remodeling reality show that was focusing solely on scaling up The Fix on Sixth. Not only did Cam think that was a freaking brilliant way to get free publicity, but the very existence of the program meant that Mina, who'd wheedled her way into an internship on the show, was in the bar almost every day, her bright smile and just-tight-enough jeans right there in front of his eyes.

The show hadn't aired yet—it was stockpiling episodes before the six-episode run launched. But one of the reasons that the producers had been keen on The Fix was the chance to include the calendar contest as a kind of backdrop to the ongoing renovation project. And, frankly, the contest had been going over like gangbusters with the regulars.

Not only were several of the male customers signing up to compete, but local fitness gurus, actors, and models were jumping on the bandwagon, too. And for the first two contests, the women had come in droves to fill the tables, drink, and cheer on the contestants.

In fact, the contest was so popular that there'd been a line around the block, and Cam had never worked so hard at his job than when he'd been behind the bar on both those Wednesdays. Honestly, he was tempted to make another more serious go at the contest, just because last Wednesday's run got him away from the bar for a solid hour during the actual competition.

"You really did that?" The shock in Darryl's voice was genuine. Prancing shirtless across a stage might be in Darryl's repertoire, but until last Wednesday, Cam had never thought it was in his. "You?" Darryl repeated. He cleared his throat, then continued in a low, booming voice. "Cameron Reed. Mild-mannered librarian by day. Internet porn star by night."

"Porn star?" Cam repeated, nodding sagely. "You know, I think it's my sparkly balls that bring in the viewers."

Nolan laughed so hard he almost spewed beer over all of them. "Librarian?"

It was Darryl's turn to laugh. "Oh, that's not part of the joke. Well, maybe the mild-mannered part."

Cam rolled his eyes. "Rare books and manuscripts," he explained to Nolan. "And Darryl loves to give me shit about it."

Like most of their friends, Darryl had assumed that Cam would take the LSAT and follow Darryl into the land of objections and depositions. But instead, Cam and his shiny, new degree in history had taken the GRE, then applied for graduate school, working toward a dual Masters in history and library science. Maybe not as sexy as trial work, but he loved the detail of it, not to mention the smell of the past, all leather and dust and paper. He'd finish at the end of the summer, and he'd already been accepted into a Ph.D. program on a really sweet scholarship.

"—can't picture you in a calendar guy contest."

Cam looked at his friend. "Sorry, what?"

"I mean the walking across the stage part. *You* I can picture," Darryl continued, obviously not realizing that Cam had lost the thread of the conversation. "Because we both know you're hot."

He swiveled to face Nolan. "Cam's my best friend—and we have a strict hands-off policy ever since I told him that I'm an equal opportunity kinda guy—but that doesn't mean I'm not allowed to comment on the quality of the merchandise. I mean, those broad shoulders? And his ridiculously tight abs? Not to mention that ass? Am I right?"

"Can't argue," Nolan said. "And I say that with a lifelong hetero record, and a tight grip on my Man Card."

"Exactly." He turned back to Cam, who was shaking his head at the ceiling as if begging help from the gods. "No question that you've got the goods. God knows you get hit on enough by customers of the female persuasion. But we both know you don't have the personality for being Mr. Pageant Guy. So what exactly made you grow those sparkly balls we've been talking about?"

"Honestly?" Cam said. "That would be your sister. She kept giving me so much grief about not entering that pretty soon everyone in the bar was asking why I didn't rip off my shirt and strut across the stage."

Darryl snorted. "Yeah, Mina can be a force of

nature when she sets her mind to it. Damn hard to resist."

He had that right.

When Mina had first suggested that Cam enter, he'd let himself believe that she was imagining him the way he thought of her—shirtless and sweaty and tangled up in the sheets. Or, at the very least, the way Darryl was describing Cam—the kind of guy that women pinned up on their walls.

But that wasn't it, and Cam knew it. Mina saw him as a friend—and all she'd been doing was yanking a friend's chain. Goading him to get out there and go a little wild. But, sadly, not with her.

Once he'd realized that there was nothing personal as far as Mina was concerned, the idea of strutting shirtless across the stage really *had* seemed daunting. But he couldn't back out without everyone at The Fix labeling him a damn pussy.

So he'd taken the coward's way out—and pretended to be a smart ass.

"Strolled down the red carpet just as smooth as you please," Nolan explained, "and then when he got up on stage, he whipped that shirt off. And there it was, spelled out in what looked like red lipstick all across his chest."

"*Comic relief,*" Darryl said, then sat back and clapped his hands together in a long, slow applause. "Fucking brilliant."

"Hey," Cam said, more than willing to suck up the praise rather than confess that his balls had shriveled, not sparkled. "Sometimes you gotta go for the laugh."

"Like I've been saying, big, sparkly balls." Nolan ran a hand through his hair. "And I need you and your balls to come on my show. That is just the kind of thing I can turn into radio gold. Especially since we can also send the show out live on social media. My fans will go nuts."

"The hell with that." A significant number of Austinites tuned in to Nolan Wood's morning drive-time radio show, *Mornings With Wood*, and Cam wasn't inclined to share his moment of lust-fueled insanity with each and every one of them.

"Where is Mina, anyway?" Cam asked, as much to change the subject as because he wanted to know. "I thought she was supposed to be running the second camera today while Brooke and Spencer work on the overflow bar."

He nodded to the far side of the room, past the maze of tables and chairs and customers, to where Brooke Hamlin and Spencer Dean—the two on-camera hosts of *The Business Plan*—made adjustments to the placement of a free-standing bar they'd finished constructing the previous evening. One of the show's two cameramen hovered nearby, filming. The second was off today, having flown back to LA to take care of a family emergency.

As the show's intern, Mina was going to be running that second camera. Except she wasn't there. And considering how much Mina had wanted this internship and how hard she'd been working, Cam couldn't quite swallow the knot of worry that had settled at the base of his throat. And when he saw the way Spencer casually stroked the back of Brooke's neck in a gesture of both affection and possession, Cam's craving to see Mina increased all the more, even though he had absolutely no right to touch her in that same gentle manner.

"Darryl?" he pressed. "Do you know where she is?"

His friend just shrugged. "I'm lucky if she remembers to send me a Christmas card. We may be twins, but the last time we were attached at the hip was—let me think—*never.*"

But Cam wasn't listening any more. Instead, he was looking out the window as the late May sun illuminated the pedestrians hurrying along the street, most of them probably heading back to work after lunch. And there, standing out like a goddess among the peasants, was Mina.

Her creamy skin seemed to glow in the sunlight, giving her an unearthly quality. She wore her dark hair short, in a pixie cut that highlighted those incredible cheekbones, and with her green eyes and long limbs, she reminded him of a young Audrey Hepburn. Growing up, his grandmother's favorite movie was *Sabrina*, and he still watched it over and over, only now he imagined himself in the role of Bogart, winning over the woman who—at first—barely even knew he existed.

She walked quickly, her eyes sparkling and a smile tugging at the corner of her mouth. She looked vibrant, happy, and Cam wondered what it was that had filled her morning with such joy. Selfishly, he wished that it were him. Even more selfishly, he hoped it wasn't another guy.

For a second, he was afraid she was going to glide right past The Fix, but then she tugged open the door and practically bounced over the threshold. She paused, glancing around, and his heart did a little flip when she met his eyes and broadened her smile. But her gaze soon traveled on, and she squealed out loud upon finding her brother.

"You're here! Why didn't you text me?" She sprinted across the bar and wrapped her brother in a hug, then yanked over an empty chair and squeezed in between Darryl and Cam.

"Because then it wouldn't be a surprise, doofus."

"Um, hello? Dad and I have known you're coming since, oh, the beginning of last semester. Not really much of a surprise."

Darryl pointed toward the doorway and then to her. "And yet may I present Exhibit A, which I like to call, *A Girl: Surprised.*"

Mina shook her head, feigning exasperation. "Whoever decided he should go to law school has a lot to answer for."

"That would be me," Darryl said.

She smiled sweetly. "I know. Beware my unexpected wrath."

Before Darryl could continue the banter—that was, frankly, making Cam a little dizzy—she shifted in her chair to include Cam and Nolan in the conversation. "Okay, quickly, quickly, because I need to get over there and help Brooke and Spencer. But tell me what you guys are talking about. I mean, right now the testosterone is so thick I can practically inhale it."

"Nosy, much?" Darryl said. "You tell us what's got you floating on clouds first."

"It shows?"

"You look like you've won the lottery," Cam said.

"I have." She laughed, then hugged herself. "You know that production studio in South Austin? The one that produces Griffin's web series?" she asked, referring to another regular at The Fix, who'd written and produced a popular podcast that had gone on to become a successful web series.

"Sure," both Darryl and Cam said in unison.

"Well, they're diving into features—Beverly Martin starred in their first one, and it's winning all sorts of awards."

"We know," Cam said. "That's why Brooke went nuts when Beverly offered to emcee the calendar contest. That's a hell of a coup having an actual movie star on the stage."

"I know," Mina continued. "And they'll be doing more movies *and* television. And guess who their newest assistant to the vice-president in charge of development will be."

"Seriously?" Darryl pulled his sister into a hug. "That's fabulous."

"I know, right? And the company is small enough I'm going to have a ton of responsibility."

"Does that mean you're not thinking about moving to LA anymore?" Darryl asked.

"Are you kidding? Hollywood's the cherry on the sundae, and I'm going to make such a splash when I get there. Especially now that I'll be going with a real resume. Not just school projects and a few internships. I mean, this job is the perfect stepping stone. A couple of years under my belt, and I'll take Hollywood by storm!"

"Congratulations," Cam said, with enough genuine enthusiasm that he didn't think twice about also engulfing her in a hug. At least not until his arms were around her, and her small breasts were pressed against his chest. He felt the shock of connection ricochet through him, and pushed away a little too fast, terrified that all that energy was about to coalesce in his cock, and give him the kind of hard on that his Wranglers really couldn't hide.

Mina, thank goodness, was still too giddy to notice his awkwardness. "I know, it's amazing. I start in a couple of weeks."

"Why not right away," Darryl asked, and Mina sighed, as if he'd asked a totally foolish question.

"Because, *hello*? I want a break. And because I'm writing that article on lighting techniques with my advisor for one of the cinematography magazines, and we still have a few tweaks. But that's outside of my coursework." She leaned back, looking smug. "I'm officially all done with school and have my MFA in film and media production to prove it."

She sighed happily as the guys applauded her. "So, what's up with y'all? Sitting over here in the corner sharing secrets?"

"More like telling stories," Darryl said. "And praising Cameron's testicles."

"Dammit, Darryl—" Cam began as he felt his face start to burn. *Shit.*

"Well, I think they must be seriously awesome," Mina said, with a wink at Cam that made the parts in question tighten pleasantly. "Is this typical guy talk? Because if it is, I don't want to ever hear another word about me discussing concealers and exfoliating scrubs with my girlfriends."

"I'm trying to convince him to come on *Mornings With Wood* to talk about his stunt last Wednesday during the contest."

"Brilliant," Mina said. "Because, personally, I'm certain there's more to the story."

"What *is* the story?" Darryl asked.

"He told me that he just wanted to do something different," Mina said. "But I think there's a woman involved." She leaned over, her hand resting on his thigh as she shoulder-bumped him. "Am I right?"

"Not even close," he lied, surprised his voice sounded normal despite the fact that his entire body felt hotter than the sun and every cell was vibrating wildly.

"I don't believe it." She leaned back, lifting her hand so she could signal for Tiffany to bring her a water. Cam drew a deep breath, grateful for the reprieve, yet frustrated by the broken contact. "I think it was all about reverse psychology."

Cam knew he'd regret it, but he couldn't help asking what she meant.

"You know," she said. "You go write something funny on your abs so that the women in the audience will notice you twice. First, to laugh, and then to say, wow, the words might be funny, but those abs are seriously awesome. I mean, right?"

She leaned toward him again, and this time Cam about leaped out of his chair when she flipped open two of the buttons on his shirt and then slid her hand inside. Her warm palm pressed against his over-heated skin, and Cam's heart started to pound so hard he was certain that she would ask if he was having a heart attack.

"Honestly, the only thing funny about your performance was you thinking this chest could be comic relief." She winked at him. "But I assumed you were being ironic."

For a second their eyes met, and her hand stilled over his heart. Her lips parted, and there was something familiar in her eyes—something hot and needy that called to him, reflecting his own violent craving.

Then she laughed lightly and withdrew her hand, and the moment faded, disappearing like dandelion seeds lost in a windstorm, and Cam was left to wonder if he'd only imagined it.

Probably so, especially since Mina was stealing a hush puppy and laughing with Darryl and Nolan and displaying absolutely no indication whatsoever that she'd felt anything real at all when she'd stroked his skin.

To Cam, though, her touch had been about as real as it gets.

"I'm right, aren't I?" she continued after she'd swallowed the hush puppy. "Cam's abs should have taken the crown." She turned to Cam, all traces of the earlier moment completely erased. "I mean, you only lost to that dude because he's a superstar reality TV show guy."

As she spoke, she grinned mischievously and hooked a thumb over her shoulder to indicate Spencer, the recently anointed Mr. February, who was approaching their table with Brooke at his side.

"Um, excuse me?" Brooke said. "Cam's no slouch, but I'm here to vouch for Spencer's abs." She waggled her eyebrows. "And the rest of him, for that matter."

"I don't even want to know," Nolan said, laughing.

"And why are we discussing my guy's abs, anyway?" Brooke asked Mina. "Especially since I'm pretty sure you're supposed to be silently subservient behind the camera."

"Subservient?" Darryl chimed in. "My little sister's never been subservient a day in her life. She wouldn't even clean her room when ordered."

"Little sister?" She pushed back from the table. "I'm fifteen minutes younger than you."

"Like I said. Shrimp."

Mina made a face, and everyone laughed. Everyone except Cam whose body was still vibrating from the contact.

"Come on," Spencer said. "We're going to anchor the new bar to the floor and the wall. Can you work the second camera?"

"Hell, yeah," Mina said, then gave a parting wave to the guys as she followed Brooke and Spencer.

"Hey, Meanie," Darryl called, using the nickname Cam knew she hated. "I'm bringing Zachary with me to my surprise party."

"You jerk. Can't you even pretend to be surprised? And who's Zachary?"

"He graduated with me, and he's doing a year with the Fifth Circuit, too, before he moves on to some humongous firm in Los Angeles. He told me his uncle's a big shot at one of the studios, and he's going to do entertainment law. He's a great guy. I think you'll like him."

Darryl had recently accepted a prestigious position as a clerk, which basically meant that he would be a Federal judge's right-hand briefing attorney for a year. Where he'd go after that, Cam knew he hadn't decided. But apparently, his friend Zach had his career path all sketched out.

"Yeah? Well, you're still a jerk. Just because he has industry access does not mean I'm going to put on a white veil and the shackles of matrimony."

Darryl held up his hands in a defensive gesture. "Not matchmaking, I swear. But the best relationships have a business bond at the core. That's what Dad always says."

"Like I'm going to take relationship advice from a guy whose marriage failed. And Mom didn't—"

"Guys," Cam interrupted, "can we agree that your dad has serious fucking clout and move on? Because I'm pretty sure Brooke and Spencer are going to fire your ass if you don't catch up with them." Probably not true, but it sounded persuasive. "And Tyree will fire me if I let my customers scare away the other customers."

"You're not on the clock," Darryl pointed out.

Cam stared him down. "I'll grab a shift if that's what it takes to stop you two bickering."

"Fair enough," Mina said, then lifted her hand, her thumb, forefinger, and pinkie on display in the sign for *I love you.*

Darryl shook his head, but flashed the sign back as she hurried across the rest of the room to help Spencer and Brooke.

Cam watched her go, thinking how easy it was to talk to her—hell, to take charge—when they were just bullshitting or talking about work. But the second he shifted his perspective and thought of her as a woman and not simply as Mina ... well, those were the times when it wasn't easy at all.

Chapter Two

"YOU'RE NOT GOING to get in trouble by blowing off work tonight?" Darryl asked as he and Mina walked the three blocks to the lot where she'd left her car.

"Nope, I'm free and clear. We work crazy late on Wednesdays with the contests, but the only work we do on Fridays and Saturdays is during the day. Brooke and Spencer figured that way we get footage, but we're out of everyone's hair on the busiest nights."

"Makes sense."

"Besides," she added, "I would have taken off just to hang out with you."

"Well, yeah. I mean that's pretty much a given." He grinned, his wide smile brightening an already handsome face. "I'm just that awesome, after all."

She bit back a smile so as not to encourage him. "Okay, awesome boy. I'm doing a 5K fun run tomorrow morning. You want to come with?"

"A 5K?"

She shrugged. "I've been thinking about training for a marathon, but a 5K's as much as I've worked up to."

"Hmm."

She glanced sideways at him as they crossed the street and headed into the pay-to-park lot. "That's an enigmatic *hmm*. You disapprove of exercise?" She looked him up and down to make her point. Her brother had been on both the swim and tennis teams all through high school, and in college, he even played water polo. He'd pushed himself through some killer workouts, and she'd been at every one of his major games, jumping up to her feet to cheer him on.

"Come on, Mina. Don't be obtuse. You know I worry about you." They'd reached the car, and he walked around to the driver's side, then held up his hand so she could toss him the keys to the small Mercedes convertible that her father had given her for her eighteenth birthday.

"There's nothing to worry about. It's just a 5K."

He didn't answer. Just snapped his fingers for the keys.

Frowning, she clicked the button to unlock the car, then got in on the passenger side. After a second, he slid into the driver's seat. "Can I have the keys, please?"

She hesitated, then dropped them in his outstretched palm. "You do realize that I've been driving for as long as you have?"

He just shrugged and slid the key into the ignition. Mina sighed, settled in, and decided not to make a thing of it. Because, honestly, she was used to it. Her father and brother had been babying her since … well, since she was a baby.

The whole thing was wackadoo as far as she was concerned. Darryl was all determined to watch out for his fragile little sister because she was weak, and he was strong and blah and blah and blah.

Except, she wasn't weak. Not any more. True, she'd been born fifteen long minutes after her brother, and they'd both been born at thirty-two weeks. Also true that he'd been exceptionally healthy for a preemie, and she'd been exceptionally weak. He'd thrived; she'd suffered from a series of medical issues and spent weeks in the NICU after her twin had gone home.

But she'd outgrown all her ailments by the time she'd hit puberty, though her parents were convinced that her petite stature—especially when compared to Darryl's robust build—stemmed from her various ailments as a kid. But so what? She was almost twenty-five now, and pretty damn cute if she said so herself. Most important, she was *fine*. Perfectly fine.

But even so, her dad and her brother pampered her. Which might be charming if it didn't mean they still saw her as weak.

Couple that with the fact that since her mom had moved out when the twins were seven, Mina had grown up in a house with two men, both of whom plunked her firmly on the Princess Throne. A seat she'd never wanted. But, at the same time, she loved her father and brother. And if they wanted to spoil her rotten…

With a sigh, she leaned back and closed her eyes,

letting Darryl steer them toward home. As annoying as he and her dad might be, the truth was there were a lot worse problems she could have than an overprotective family.

Like, she thought, one that dabbled in matchmaking.

She frowned, suddenly suspicious, and opened her eyes. "Tonight's just us, right? You didn't invite Zacharius over, did you? Because I want to put on some yoga pants, make some popcorn, and veg."

"It's Zachary, and no. Just us."

"Good." She felt the stress practically ooze off her. "Are we watching at my place or Dad's?"

"Let's do the house," Darryl said. "I may crash early."

"Sounds good." Her father still lived in the house they grew up in, and Darryl's room had stayed the same during his years in undergrad and law school, like a museum in honor of the departing hero. Mina had moved out, too, but she'd taken her stuff with her. Not far, though. Unlike her brother, who'd moved out of state, Mina had not only stayed in Texas, she'd stayed in Austin for both undergrad and graduate school.

She'd lived on campus until she got her bachelor's, but the summer before grad school, she'd moved into the family's garage apartment. A well-appointed residence, it took up the entire second floor of the detached six car garage that graced the back half of the five-acre lot nestled in the hills near Lake Austin.

It had been her father's suggestion—another nod to taking care of little Mina. But by that time she'd spent four years with a roommate and had learned the value of a rent-free place to live. Especially one with access to a pool, tennis court, theater room, and a seriously well-stocked wine cellar.

"How long are you staying with Dad?" Mina asked as Darryl turned the car up the private drive that led to their gate.

"Not sure," he said. "It's a big house. If he doesn't drive me too crazy, I might stay for the year of my clerkship, then see where I land."

"Good," she said. "You might be a jerk on occasion, but I've missed having you around."

He pulled the car up in front of the massive garage and killed the engine. "Glad I'm back, too," he said. "Meet at the house at six? I'll order Chinese."

"Perfect." She reached for the car door.

"Oh, to finish answering your question, I did invite one person over for movie night."

Her hand stilled, and she groaned as she turned to her brother. "Please tell me you're joking. It's Friday. It's been a long week. All I want is to kick back and chill, not act all perky for some guy you're looking to fix me up with."

He laughed. "It's only Cam. I told him to come by for Chinese and whatever movie you saddle us with— see? I didn't forget that it's your turn to pick. Or should I tell him not to come over?"

"Cam?" She realized she was smiling and dialed it back. "Well, duh. Of course, Cam's welcome."

"Just checking," Darryl said. "God forbid I foist a guy on you."

"Oh, please." She pushed open the car door, using the motion to camouflage the fact that she'd turned her face away. "Cam's not a guy. He's practically like family."

Which completely begged the question of why her skin suddenly burned with the memory of his bare chest under her palm—or why she had a sudden urge to spend the rest of the afternoon taking a scented bath, shaving her legs, and trying on outfits until she found something casual yet cute, and just a tiny bit sexy.

LIKE FAMILY?

Hours later, her words still rang in her head, and she wondered at her own foolishness. Because no way in hell was Cam like family.

Not tonight. Not now.

Not while Mina was standing in front of her bathroom mirror in her underwear, her entire body tingling as she let her mind drift back on the afternoon. The pressure of Cam's body against hers as he hugged her in congratulations. The heat of his skin when she'd so boldly slid her hand in his shirt. The blood pounding under her fingers and the way she'd felt that unexpected craving rush through her as if following a path from her fingertips all the way down to her sex.

With a little shiver, she eased her fingers under the

band of her panties, then moaned when she realized that she was wet.

A heartbeat later, her eyes flew open and she jumped backward, pulling her hand free like some kid caught in bed with a dirty magazine.

Good grief, she hadn't even realized what she'd been doing. Her hand stroking down her abdomen, her fingers seeking her heat. And her mind lost in the memory of Cam's innocent touch, while her reaction to it had been anything but innocent.

Honestly, what the devil was wrong with her?

That, thank goodness, was an easy question to answer.

She'd been working too hard. She needed to get out. Have some fun. Enjoy some male companionship of the non-Cameron variety. Because she *really* wasn't interested in him that way. He was Darryl's best friend, for one thing. And he'd been such a fixture in her household growing up, that he was practically a second brother.

Plus, she saw him at The Fix all the time, so they certainly couldn't start something. How awkward would that be when it inevitably ended? And it *would* end, because Mina wasn't even remotely interested in getting serious about a guy. Not now, when she was just getting her career off the ground and proving to her father and brother—not to mention herself—that she was more than capable of successfully managing her own life.

Besides, Cam was too damn nice, and Mina gravitated to men with a little bit of an edge. The kind of guy who grabbed control and made a woman melt. And as much as she adored Cam, he was probably the least edgy guy that she knew.

Now, though, he was in her head, which meant that movie night was definitely going to lean toward awkward.

She sighed, then snatched up her phone and dialed, determined to erase all thoughts of her brother's best friend.

"If it isn't the lovely Mina." Jeff answered on the first ring, his voice as smooth and flirtatious as always. "How are you, beautiful?"

"Feeling claustrophobic in these walls. I'm hanging out with my brother this evening, but I thought I might go out and hit some clubs around eleven."

"And you're looking for company?" His tone made clear that he understood perfectly what kind of company she sought. The kind that started with drinks and a loud beat and sweaty gyrations, and then ended up with more sweat, moans, and gyrations of the horizontal variety. The kind of company that was never serious but always fun, and that could capture a girl's attention long enough to erase everything else—or every*one* else—from her mind.

She'd met Jeff during her first year of grad school at a friend's Super Bowl party. There'd been definite sparks between them, but not much more, and after a couple of dates they'd drifted apart. But then he'd called her a few months later when he'd ended up with an extra ticket to a red carpet movie premiere in Austin. She'd jumped at the chance, and after being fueled up with much champagne, they'd both jumped on each other.

It wasn't serious. It wasn't even frequent. But somehow without ever really discussing it, they'd ended up in that elusive land of fuck buddies. Or friends with benefits.

In other words, exactly the kind of distraction between the sheets that Mina knew she needed. Because if she was spending the evening in her dad's theater room with Cam—if her mind was going to be constantly drifting back to the way his skin felt against hers—then by the time the movie was over, she was going to be in serious need of some big-time distracting.

"SOMETHING MINDLESS WITH A LOT OF ACTION," Darryl suggested as he pushed the lever to recline one end of the leather sofa.

"Works for me," Cam said, carrying a bowl of popcorn toward the couch. They'd already done significant damage to the Chinese take-out. Now, they were moving on to traditional movie snacks. Darryl had even brought a box of Junior Mints. "Or we could go the classic route. Like maybe *Rear Window?*" He settled on the end opposite from Darryl. That side didn't recline, but he stretched out, propping his feet up on the ottoman.

Mina swallowed, realizing that put her in the middle. Not a surprise, since those were the trio's usual movie-watching spots. But today it seemed too close for comfort. Especially since she'd be sharing the ottoman with Cam.

Which, she told herself sternly, was *No. Big. Deal.*

"Yo. Meanie?" Darryl prompted, making her jump.

"Sorry. Mind wandering. I'm always good with Hitchcock." Just last semester she'd written a paper on the development of Hitchcock's work over the course of his career. "But I was kind of hoping for *Good Will Hunting.*"

Both men stared at her as if she'd lost her mind, and she took a step back, holding up her hands to ward off their blatant disdain. "Just a thought," she said. "I mean, it is my turn to pick, right? Besides, it's a good movie, and I want to reference it in a lecture I'm giving to some undergrads next week."

"Math in movies?" Darryl quipped.

"Character and theme in love stories, actually." Although maybe something without a hint of romance or sex would be the better choice.

"Veto," Cam said, while Darryl nodded.

"You wanna watch the latest *Fast and Furious*, I'm all over that shit," Darryl said. "I'll even sit back and chill to *North by Northwest*. But chick flicks are out."

"Why do I even hang with you two?" She didn't bother waiting for an answer, just grabbed a beer from the mini-fridge, then plopped down in her usual spot between them. The house was old enough that the theater room wasn't original. Her dad had converted one of several dens, and in the process, he'd decided to forego individual theater-style chairs for the front-and-center sofa and a couple of recliners on risers behind it.

The sofa, he said, was perfect for a family of three. And growing up, Darryl, Mina, and Cam had gotten in the habit of sharing it, just as the twins had done with their dad.

Today, Mina wished that she'd taken a recliner for herself. Already, she was far too aware of Cam right next to her.

She told herself to chill. She'd watch the movie, drink a beer, then meet Jeff and work this overwhelming horniness out of her system.

And the guys were right. Hitchcock was the much better choice.

"I never figured out *Good Will Hunting*," Cam said. "I mean, he drops his whole life and leaves his family to run off across the country, chasing this girl when he doesn't even know if it's going to work out."

"Leaves his family?" Mina said. "He was an orphan."

"His friends *were* his family," Cam said with such intensity that her heart twisted. She knew Cam's story. He'd grown up with his grandmother and sister because both his mother and father had walked out.

"Well, I think it's romantic," she said. "He was taking a risk for love. That was the point."

"And what about her?" Cam continued. "When he lands on her doorstep, how is he going to know if she really wants him there, or if she just feels obligated since he gave up everything to follow her?"

"Dude," Darryl said, "you have way over-analyzed that movie."

"Maybe Cam should give my lecture," Mina joked, resisting the urge to reach over and squeeze his hand. She might be delving too deep into pop psychology, but she couldn't help but think that Cam saw his own life in that movie.

"Hitchcock," Cam said. "I'm putting my foot down."

"You're sexy when you're commanding," Darryl joked, making Mina roll her eyes even though, silently, she kind of agreed.

Ultimately, they settled on *Psycho*, and even though it was tame by modern standards—and even though Mina had seen it dozens of times—she still cringed and pulled up her afghan during the infamous shower scene. And when she finally relaxed and stretched out again, her feet bumped into Cam's on the ottoman.

She jumped, still edgy from the scene, and he grinned at her. "What? You think I'm going to attack?"

"I think you're on my side of the footstool."

"Your side? Girl, you gave it up when you abandoned the ottoman during your scream-a-thon." He gave her shin a light kick. "This ottoman is mine now. The United Ottoman of Cameron."

She kicked him back. "Not hardly," she said, then squealed when he shoved her feet toward the edge, setting them both off into a full-fledged foot war for ownership of ottoman. A war so intense and hard-fought that they were both laughing so much they didn't even hear Darryl until he finally paused the movie.

"You two going to play footsies all night, or do you wanna finish the flick?"

She froze—her legs twined with Cameron's as their hands also battled for ownership of the afghan that now covered them both. It was fun and intimate and just a little sweet.

A few days ago, she would have thought nothing of it.

Tonight, though…

Tonight, his heavy breathing seemed sensual, not the result of silly exertion. And the fire in his eyes suggested passion, not playfulness. She was seeing him in ways she shouldn't—in ways that were pure fantasy.

Oh, no…

A split second later, she'd untangled herself and all but leaped to the middle of the couch.

Cam, she noticed, had done the same, launching himself the opposite direction so that he was practically sitting on the armrest.

"Sorry," she said to Darryl. "Just screwing around. *Fooling* around, I mean. Just being a goof." Thank God it was dark because her cheeks felt on fire.

"Start the movie," Cam said, and Mina had no idea if he looked at her or Darryl because her eyes were locked straight ahead on the screen.

By the time the final credits rolled, Mina's heart rate and breathing had settled again, but she'd processed none of the movie. Thank goodness she'd seen it a zillion times, because if anyone walked in now and asked her to recite the plot, the moving pictures that had flashed across the screen for the last couple of hours would have been no help whatsoever.

"It's almost ten," Cam said, "and I'm starving. You guys want to grab a late bite? I'm thinking pancakes at Magnolia." The twenty-four-hour eatery had two locations, one just a few miles from the house.

"Honestly, I'm beat," Darryl said. "But I'll take a rain check for sometime this weekend."

"Okay by me," Cam said, his attention shifting to Mina. "How about you? Does the idea of a gingerbread pancake tickle your fancy?"

"Always," she said. "But I can't." She swallowed, feeling weirdly disloyal. "I, um, promised a friend I'd meet him for a drink. Maybe go dancing. You know. Friday night and all that."

"Uh-huh," Darryl said, hoisting himself off the couch and then grabbing the wallet he'd left on one of the side tables. He opened it, then tossed her a condom packet, his mouth curved into a wicked grin. "Wouldn't be a good big brother if I didn't remind you to be responsible."

"You mean you wouldn't be an asshole," she said, and as she tossed it back to him, she realized that her cheeks were burning. Which was stupid. She was a grown woman. If she wanted to go out on a date—hell, if she wanted to have sex with her date—she could totally do that.

But despite her righteous indignation, after Cam had

left, and Mina had returned to the apartment, she found herself dialing Jeff's number and canceling, claiming that she was too tired to go out.

"Well, damn, baby. I was looking forward to a tumble."

"Would be nice," she agreed. But the truth was, it wasn't Jeff she wanted to tumble with.

With a sigh, she started to unbutton her jeans, planning to change into her PJ's. But her hand stilled before she'd even pulled down the zipper. Because maybe, just maybe, she was in the mood for pancakes after all.

Chapter Three

MINA LEANED against the doorjamb and tapped on her brother's door. "It's me. Can I come in?"

"When have I ever kept you out?"

"A valid point." Growing up, they'd had connecting bedrooms, and they'd only ever shut the door on rare occasions. And since the idea of sneaking a date in under their strict father's roof bordered on insane, they'd never been the kind of siblings who'd kept the other out with a ribbon tied on the doorknob or some other symbol.

She edged inside and found him sitting in his recliner with a book in his hand. She sat on the edge of the bed, then wondered what the hell she was doing there, anyway.

"Bored?" he asked as the silence lingered.

"I canceled Jeff," she said, then added, "My date," as if that wasn't obvious. "But now I'm peckish. I keep thinking about those pancakes Cam suggested."

"Uh-huh," he said, and even though it was a perfectly tame comment, she had to bite her tongue to keep from asking what he meant by that. Instead, she calmly asked if he wanted to go to Magnolia with her.

Not that she needed a chaperone. She just wanted company. After all, it had been years since she and her brother had been able to simply hang out together. This was a perfect opportunity.

"Pancakes," he said, shutting his book and looking at her intently. So intently it seemed as though he was looking straight into her mind. Hell, he probably was. Maybe it was a twin thing, but Darryl always had been able to read her.

Which begged the question of why she'd come here in the first place since Darryl was the last person she wanted to know about her lust-filled Cameron thoughts.

"Look, it's a simple question." She heard the snappishness in her voice, but couldn't seem to dial it back. "Do you want to come or not?"

"If you're looking for company, you know I'll join you."

Of course, he would. She exhaled, feeling both ridiculous and guilty. She knew damn well that he was beat and wanted to stay in and chill. She also knew that all she had to do was snap her fingers and he'd do what she asked. Their father, too.

That's what came of being the sickly second twin. Her father pampered her to make up for not having spawned a perfect pair. And Darryl doted on her because he blamed himself for her rough beginning—as if a twin in utero could be culpable for taking up more than his fair share of their uterine condo and amenities.

And even if he had been intentionally hogging the amniotic fluid, she was fine now. All good. Time to move on.

But that went for her as well as him. If she wanted him to stop babying her, then maybe it was time for her to stop hinting that she needed to be babied.

"You know what? Never mind."

He settled back in the recliner. "Never mind?"

"Yeah, it's fine. Besides, you should crash soon. Aren't you having brunch with the judge and the other clerks tomorrow morning?"

"Not until eleven."

"Still." She shrugged. "Seriously. I'm good. I'll just make some toast, then crawl into bed and read." She flashed a sassy grin. "Just like my big brother."

As she hoped, he laughed. She gave him a quick hug, said goodnight, then sent her dad a text message wishing him a good night, too. In the seventies, Bruce Silver had founded a local organic grocery store that had grown into a nationwide chain worth millions of dollars. Now, her dad tended to live on the road. Right now, she was pretty sure he was in Portland.

She hesitated, then sent her mom a text, as well. Alicia Silver had moved to Oklahoma right before the twins graduated high school. She'd never gone to college, and when the cost of living in Austin had gotten too high for her, she'd gone to work in her uncle's feed store outside of Enid. She called Mina every week or so, then listened with rapt attention as Mina told her about the work she did for Griffin and his awesome web series, or about being an intern for *The Business Plan* at The Fix. Tonight, she texted her mom about her job offer.

The response came back right away—*That's my girl. You're going to make me proud.*

Mina smiled, but it was bittersweet. Never did her mom say that she *did* make her proud. Just that maybe, in some far off distant time, Alicia would look back at her daughter, nod, and think, *that's it. Now, she's done it.*

And she would, too. Dammit, Mina was going to make Alicia and Darryl and her father proud. She was going to prove that she wasn't a fragile little thing any more. She was strong, and she was smart. Maybe she wasn't a lawyer or a corporate big shot, but she was going to make it big.

Hell, yeah, she would.

Inside the guest house, she hesitated by the door. Why shouldn't she go to Magnolia and have pancakes with Cam? They were friends, weren't they? And since all she'd had this evening was popcorn and Chinese, she really was hungry.

Before she could talk herself out of it, she grabbed her purse and keys off the small table by the front door, then headed for her car.

It only took a few minutes to get to Magnolia, but as she searched in vain for a parking space, her nerve faded. She told herself she wasn't nervous about seeing Cam—why on earth would she be?—she was just frustrated by the lack of parking. But, honestly, she should have known better on a Friday night.

Maybe she should blow off pancakes and go to The Fix instead.

After all, if company was what she craved, she'd find it in spades there. And since she knew Cam was elsewhere, it would be a totally distraction-free evening.

She'd get a drink, grab a bite, maybe hang out with Brooke, who Mina had really come to admire. And she wanted to ask Brent how he was doing with finding a babysitter. She knew his regular sitter had quit unexpectedly just yesterday, and she wanted to tell him that she'd help out whenever she could.

The thoughts zipped through her head as she drove downtown, then walked the short distance from the parking lot to The Fix, the Friday night crowd on Sixth Street jostling around her.

The irony was that she'd never been big on babysitting. But her offer wasn't about Brent or even about his daughter, Faith. It was about the atmosphere at The Fix. She'd known when she begged for the internship that she'd like the television work, but she hadn't expected how much she'd love sliding in as a regular at the bar. But she did. It felt good there.

Hell, it felt like a home. Like family. A place where she could kick back and completely relax. And tonight, that was exactly what she needed.

Then she tugged open the door, stepped inside, and realized that was bullshit. There'd be no relaxing for her tonight. Not here. Because there was Cam, sitting at the bar and laughing his ass off while Eric poured him a fresh drink, and Matthew Herrington banged his hand on the bar as if to emphasize a punchline.

For a moment, Mina considered just backing out the door. Then she mentally shored up her big girl panties, pushed her way inside, and marched straight toward Cameron.

"Hey, Loser," she said, giving him a light smack on the shoulder.

"Ow." He twisted around, his smile widening when he saw it was her. "What was that for?"

Because I can't get the memory of the way your skin felt against my fingers out of my head.

"Because you're supposed to be at Magnolia Cafe. Good thing I didn't go in search of you and a pancake," she said.

"Pancakes and coffee felt too tame. I decided I needed a drink." He held up what looked like bourbon and water. "What can I say? I was in the mood to get a little buzzed."

"Not too buzzed," Matthew said as he slipped off his stool. "I've got you in my book for noon tomorrow."

"His book?"

"Personal training," Cam said.

"Tomorrow," Matthew said, pointing a stern finger at Cam before nodding to Mina and disappearing into the crowd gathered in front of the stage where a local band was about to start another set.

"I've seen him around the bar dozens of times," Mina said. "I never thought to ask what he does."

"He owns the gym over on Lavaca," Cam said, pointing roughly toward the west. "I've been working with him for a couple of months now."

"I can tell," she said, then immediately regretted it when his brows rose.

"Yeah? Guess it's good to know I'm getting my money's worth." He nodded toward Matthew's recently vacated seat, and she climbed up on the stool, happy to have been invited.

She hesitated for a second, then decided to face the elephant in the room head-on. "If what I touched was any indication, your money is very well spent."

He looked up, his head slightly cocked and his blue-gray eyes locked on hers. For a moment, time simply froze. Then he reached for his drink and took a long swallow. "What happened to your date?" he finally asked.

She lifted a shoulder. "I canceled. I wasn't in the mood."

"And yet here you are."

She swallowed, her mouth going dry as a shiver rippled up her spine. "Here I am."

"Are you in the mood for a drink?"

"Yeah," she said, matching his smile. "I think a drink sounds like a really great idea."

Chapter Four

CAM LIFTED A HAND, signaling for Eric, who finished pouring a martini for a blonde at the far end of the bar, then came down to Cam and Mina's end. "Another?" Eric asked, nodding at Cam's half-full drink.

Cam nodded, then downed the last of the bourbon and water in one swallow. Because with Mina right there beside him, he needed all the courage he could gather, liquid or otherwise. "And something for Mina, too," he said. "A dirty martini with the blue cheese olives?" He'd taken her order enough to know that was one of her favorite drinks.

"Not tonight," she said. "Just a glass of wine. Let's do a Pinot Noir," she told Eric. "You pick the label."

"You got it," Eric said.

"Not your usual," Cam said as soon as Eric returned with their drinks.

She took a sip, then nodded approval before turning

to him with the hint of a smile. "Maybe I want to keep my wits tonight."

The smile widened, revealing a small dimple that Cam thought was about the sexiest thing he'd ever seen. He forced himself to look away, concentrating on his bourbon and kicking himself for ordering the second one. Because right then he was feeling far too bold. And he was still sober enough to worry about making a complete and total ass of himself.

After all, it wasn't as if she'd come to The Fix looking for him. She'd come because she worked there. Because she wanted to have a drink and see her friends.

Cam didn't even factor into the equation.

But she's sitting next to you now, the little devil on his shoulder said. And, dammit, the little devil was right.

Too bad Cam wasn't entirely sure what to do about that interesting reality.

For a moment, silence hung between them. Then he stood, his feet balanced on the crossbar of the stool as he leaned over the bar and grabbed a menu from the prep area. "We should get food," he said, in response to her raised eyebrows.

"You need to look at the menu? How long have you worked here?"

He shot her a sideways glance. "I thought you might want to take a look." He tossed the menu, unopened, back into the work area. "But never mind. I'll order for both of us."

"A man who takes charge." She took a sip of her Pinot Noir, then settled back on her stool. "I like it."

He knew she was teasing, of course, but that didn't change the fact that her words seemed to fill the air between them, buzzing and humming with unexplored potential.

He drew another breath and told himself to quell the fantasies. This was just Mina. And she didn't see him as anyone other than just Cam.

Once again he lifted his hand to get Eric's attention. "Spinach and Mushroom Risotto Balls along with the Cheeseburger Fries." He flashed a grin toward Mina. "Friday night food."

"Hell, yeah," she said, as the warm glow of her approval filled him.

Good God, he had it bad.

Eric put in the order, Cam and Mina sipped their drinks, and the band finished out their current number, a rockabilly tune that had the place hopping.

Mina had shifted in her chair to watch, but now that the band had finished the number, she turned back to sip her drink.

He expected her to say something, but she stayed quiet, her fingertip tracing around the rim of her glass as she looked from her wine, to him, and then around at the other customers.

Silence filled the space between them, a gaping maw that mocked him, making uncertainty twist in his stomach until he had to shift on the stool, trying to relieve some of the pressure of the moment.

He was being an idiot, of course. How many times had they sat quietly together? Hundreds, surely. And the quiet was never uncomfortable. So why was the silence suddenly so heavy? Why did he feel as if he had to say something smart or funny or ironic or interesting?

And for that matter, *what* could he say?

He didn't know, but he'd reached the point where if he didn't say something his head really might explode, so he dove in with, "So——"

And at exactly the same moment, she said, "You know——"

Their eyes met, a moment passed, and then they both burst out laughing.

"You go first," she said. "What were you going to say?"

He finished his drink and shook his head. "Honestly? I have no idea. You?"

Her lips twitched. "Not a clue," she admitted, and they both started laughing again.

"I'm starving," she said. "And that's not what I planned to say, but it's true." She leaned over and brushed her shoulder against him, but whether she was being friendly or flirty, he had no idea. "Thanks for ordering food."

"Well, I figured what with you missing out on your pancakes…"

"This is better," she said. "If I'd gone to Magnolia, you wouldn't have been there." She met his eyes, and for a moment it seemed as if he'd been swallowed up by the emerald fire of her gaze.

"Yeah," he finally said, impressed that he could form words. "This is much better."

This time the silence between them didn't seem awkward at all. This time, it seemed full of possibility.

All too soon, Eric sidled up and put the order in front of them. And suddenly Cam didn't give a flip about food. He just wanted to hit rewind and keep playing those few moments when it was just the two of them, their eyes locked on each other as if nothing else existed in the world.

"This looks amazing," Mina said, oblivious to the spell that had been broken. She reached for a fry, then moaned with pleasure after she tasted it.

The sound cut straight through Cam, firing his senses. He watched her, his entire body on edge as she licked her fingertips, then closed her eyes to savor the food before releasing a deep, satisfied sigh.

After a moment, she opened her eyes and grinned at him. "You're not eating?"

"Believe me, I'm doing just fine."

Her cheeks flushed. "Oh." She plucked up a risotto ball, then held it out to him. "These are amazing. Want a bite?"

Oh, yes.

"Sure," he said, and she held it to his mouth. He bit down, his lips brushing her fingertips. And as they did, she ran her teeth over her lower lip. Honestly, it was a freaking miracle that he didn't come right then.

He'd always heard people talk about how sensual eating could be, but until tonight Cam hadn't understood what that meant.

Trouble was, he still wasn't sure if this was a one-sided fantasy...or if Mina was finally seeing him the way that he'd always seen her.

He opened his mouth to finish the risotto ball, only to see her pop the remaining half into her own mouth.

"Good," she said.

"Very." He nodded toward the plate. "I'd take another." He held his breath, waiting for her to lift one to his lips. But all she did was smile and push the plate toward him.

She took a sip of wine, then cleared her throat. "So, are you going to do that show with Nolan?"

It took him a second to figure out what she was talking about. "Morning drive time to talk about words scrawled on my chest? I'm thinking not."

"Oh, you should. And I could go with you."

That surprised him. "You could? Why?"

"I could take the handheld camera, and we could film it. Then use the clips to advertise the contest, the bar. It would be great. I bet a snippet would even end up in Brooke and Spencer's show."

"Yeah, you know, it's not really my dream to be plastered all over television."

Her eyes widened as her brows rose. "A little late for that, don't you think? You know they're going to include your stunt during the contest when the first episode airs. It's a hoot and you're standing right on the new stage. And the first episode's going to focus on designing and constructing that stage."

"They've told you that? About my chest, I mean?"

"No, but isn't it obvious?"

He supposed it was. *The Business Plan* was a show about doing renovations and remodeling at *The Fix*, but the producers had been excited about having the contest in the background. Which meant Mina was right; his little stunt was exactly the kind of thing they'd use in previews and teasers for the show. Which meant that his moment of self-deprecation was about to be splashed across televisions all over the country.

Oh, joy.

"Actually, I have a better idea," Mina said. "You should go on Nolan's show after you win Mr. March. You know, from comic relief to calendar beefcake."

He shook his head laughing. "Oh, no. I'm not entering the March contest. Not happening." And not even the fact that she'd more or less admitted that he looked good shirtless was going to make him change his mind.

Beefcake. Honestly, coming from Mina's lips it had a nice little ring to it.

"Oh, come on," she cajoled. "You should. Shouldn't he enter the next contest?" she asked, tilting her head up to aim the question not at Cam but at someone who'd apparently come up behind him.

He swiveled to find Brent moving around to stand between him and Mina. "He should," Brent said, his blue eyes flat and hard. "Absolutely, he should."

"What? I—"

Brent tilted his head, his eyes locked on Cam. "Don't you support the place that employs you?"

Cam looked between him and Mina. "I—well, yeah. Sure, but—"

Brent burst out laughing. "Sorry, I couldn't stay stoic any longer."

"Asshole." Cam tossed a wadded up cocktail napkin at him.

"It was the look on your face. I couldn't pass up giving you shit." He pointed at Cam. "But you really should enter. I happen to know you ran a close second."

"Why don't you enter?" Cam shot back.

"Um, yeah, no."

Cam leaned back on his stool. "I rest my case."

Brent just shook his head, then turned his attention to Mina. "Listen, I came over to tell you not to walk to your car alone. Four women have had their purses snatched in the area over the last two days."

"Yikes."

"I'll walk her to her car," Cam said, eyeing Mina. He expected her to protest—he'd seen her shrug off Darryl's constant care—but whether because of Brent's warning or something else, she just nodded and said that sounded great.

And then, when she added that she'd give him a ride home, he thought the bottom might actually fall out of his stomach.

She pointed to her almost empty glass of wine. "This is all I'm having tonight, and I'm guessing you got here in a ride share?"

"I have the most perfect parking spot near my place," he said, making her laugh. It was a longstanding joke between him and Darryl. During undergrad it had been a constant battle between the two to see who'd get cajoled into taking out their car first, and sacrificing whatever primo parking place they'd managed to score near the apartment they'd shared.

"Besides," he added, pointing to his glass, "I've had three of these, I think. So it's just as well that you're here to babysit me on my way home."

"Is that so?" She leaned toward him, mischief flashing in her eyes as she rested a hand on his thigh for balance. "Just how much care are you going to need?"

Was she flirting? Holy shit, she was flirting.

It must have surprised her as much as it did him, because she sat back suddenly, her eyes wide, then cleared her throat. "Um, sorry. I—I forgot to ask Brent something."

Before he could ask what, she hopped down and hurried toward the back, following Brent's path through the crowd.

Eric came over and leaned against the bar, looking frazzled. At the other end, Aly was mixing drinks, too, having recently started to split her time between waiting tables and bartending.

"You want another?" Eric asked. "Better yet, you want to hop back here and help out. Aly's good, but slow. Tonight's not a good night for slow."

"Not a chance," Cam said. "And just remember that the more crowded the bar, the more likely we'll all still have a job come December." That, Cam knew, was the drop-dead date. He didn't know how much money The

Fix needed to show on the books, but he knew that if the magic number hadn't been reached by New Year's Eve, then Tyree and the partners were selling the place.

Honestly, the thought was too depressing to ponder.

"Another?" Eric prompted, and Cam glanced around for Mina, his mind recalling that sparkle in her eye when she'd pressed her hand to his thigh.

He imagined pulling her close and kissing her hard. And he considered the very interesting fact that Eric was offering him another shot of liquid courage.

And what the hell, right? After all, he did have a ride home.

"You know what?" he said. "I do want another."

Eric's grin suggested he'd seen every one of Cam's thoughts flash across his face, but to his credit he didn't say a word. Just poured the bourbon, added some water, and slid the drink across the bar to Cam, who sipped. And then sipped some more.

A few more sips, and he was almost to the bottom of the glass. And Mina still hadn't come back.

He frowned, unwelcome jealousies popping into his head. What if she'd run into one of her old boyfriends? What if she'd settled in at someone else's table? It wasn't as if they were together. And, sure, she offered him a ride, but that didn't obligate her to stay attached to his hip. Did it?

He twisted at the waist, his gaze skimming the crowd, and almost sagged with relief when he saw her pushing her way toward him, her hand going up in greeting.

"Sorry," she said as she reached him. "It took a while to catch up to Brent, and I had to hit the ladies room."

His attention was drawn to her mouth, the lips pale pink and glossy. She'd freshened her makeup. But had she freshened it for him?

That green thread of jealousy returned along with the memory of Brent's face. "What did you need to talk to Brent about?" He worked to keep his voice casual. It hadn't occurred to him before, but Brent was single. And good-looking.

Not that Cam considered himself an expert on the appeal of men, but he'd seen the reactions of enough female customers to confirm the assessment.

Were Brent and Mina—?

He forced himself not to think about it. Mostly because the thought made him want to find Brent and punch him.

"Mrs. Westerfield quit," Mina said.

"Who?"

"His babysitter," Mina explained. "I offered to babysit if he needs someone. Assuming it works into my schedule."

"Yeah? That was nice of you."

She laughed. "Well, don't sound so surprised!"

"Sorry. I only mean that you never babysat. When we were in high school, I mean. Did you?" He assumed he knew, but they hadn't gone to the same high school. For all Cam knew, Mina had been a babysitting fiend.

She lifted a shoulder in a casual shrug. "How hard can it be? She's five. No baby food, no diapers."

"And tons of energy."

She crossed her arms over her chest and stared down her nose at him. "Okay, mister. What do you know about it?"

"More than you, apparently," he teased. "I used to babysit every Wednesday and Friday in high school."

"Seriously?"

"We needed the money." He spoke the words flatly, without any editorial tone. His life was what it was, and it was a hell of a lot different than Darryl and Mina's. But she knew that as well as he did.

Cam and Darryl had met in a park near Cam's house the summer after second grade. Darryl and Mina were spending June with their mother, who was downwardly mobile after her divorce, and who'd moved into a small house one block over from where Cam and Kiki lived with their grandmother.

They'd become fast-friends, albeit mostly summer ones.

"Do you remember Mrs. Waring?" Cam asked.

"Sure. She lived at the end of Mom's block. She had what, three kids?"

"Four. And her husband died when the youngest was five months."

"You sat for them?"

He spread his hands. "Closer than riding my bike to Whataburger and flipping meat patties."

"Hmm," she said, pursing her lips as she studied him.

"What?"

"Got any plans for Sunday?"

If he did, he'd cancel them. But he played it cool. "Why?"

"Because Brent has a meeting here all morning about the renovations, and then after that he has a date."

"Really? With who?"

"No idea. He said Jenna fixed him up."

As far as Cam knew, Jenna, Reece, and Brent had been best friends since about the dawn of time. And now that Jenna and Reece were a couple, Cam was certain that Jenna was trying to find a girl for Brent—whether Brent wanted one or not.

"Let me guess—he asked you to watch Faith."

"And wouldn't it be great if I had someone with experience by my side? Could you? Are you working?"

"I'm not sure, actually." He'd just been promoted to the assistant weekend manager position, and Tyree had given him tomorrow off to chill and enjoy. But when Cam had last checked, Tyree hadn't posted Sunday's schedule.

He glanced around for the owner, but didn't see him in the crowd. And considering what a big man Tyree was, that probably meant he was in the office.

"Hey, Mike," he said to the eighteen-year-old bar back who was unloading the freshly washed bar glasses from a green plastic rack. "When you head back to the kitchen, could you pop your head in the office and tell Tyree I have a question?"

"Sure," Mike said, flashing a quick grin that so resembled Reece that it reminded Cam that the two were family. Cousins, actually. And apparently close ones.

A few minutes later, Mike was gone, but then Tyree re-appeared in his place. "Sunday? Yeah, you're on from four to close."

"Oh." His eyes cut to Mina, then back to Tyree. "No problem."

Tyree's eyes narrowed almost imperceptibly. "But I was about to go into the schedule and change that. I'll already be here because of the meeting, and Jenna said she's working late Sunday night, too."

Cam said nothing, afraid to get his hopes up.

"Tell you what. Consider this your last responsibility-free weekend. And next Friday night, you'll dive into your new position with lots of vim and vigor. Deal?"

"Sounds perfect to me," Cam said, forcing himself to look only at Tyree and not grin like an idiot at Mina.

Tyree nodded, the firm motion sealing the deal. And that's when Cam turned to Mina. "Looks like I'm all yours."

"That's fabulous," she said.

"We're going to babysit Faith for Brent," Cam explained, since Tyree was still standing there.

"Uh-huh," Ty said, glancing from Cam to Mina and then back to Cam again. "Well, you have fun, son." And then after a slight pause he met Cam's eyes. "With Faith."

Cam nodded in acknowledgement. He appreciated the show of male solidarity, but was going to feel like a damn fool if this was all in his imagination. If there was no connection.

Or if he never got up enough goddamn nerve to even hint to Mina how he felt.

Then again, he'd already inadvertently dropped a hundred hints. Tyree had seen that clearly enough.

Had Mina?

And if she had, was she ignoring them?

Hell. His stomach twisted again, and suddenly his twenty-four years felt much more like fourteen.

He rarely dated because he didn't have time. And, honestly, because the women he met didn't send the same thrill running through his blood that Mina did.

But right then he was wishing he'd had just a little more practice in the art of reading a woman.

On stage, the band started to play a cover of Taylor Swift's *Love Story.* He'd been fourteen when the song came out, and every time he heard Swift belting out the ballad about two kids in love, he'd thought of Mina.

Beside him, Mina pushed her wine glass away. "It's getting late. I should probably head home."

"Right. Sure. Just let me pay, and we can go." He signaled to Eric, then settled the bill. They said a few goodbyes as they headed for the door, and she led the way, heading east on Sixth Street and then turning south on one of the streets that ran perpendicular.

They walked for several blocks, the streets becoming darker and more deserted.

"Did you park all the way across the river?" Cam asked after they'd gone three blocks.

"Ha, ha. The closer lot was full. But I'm just over there." She pointed down the street where a small sign with an arrow advertised paid parking.

They kept walking, but then she stopped and turned, obviously in response to the pounding footsteps that Cam had also heard.

It was a guy in a hoodie, and by the time Cam turned, he was practically on top of them. He shoved Mina into Cam, sending him stumbling. And as he righted himself, he realized that the sharp noise in the air was the echo of Mina's scream.

"Mina!"

She swallowed the scream, her eyes wide. "My purse! That fucker cut the strap on my purse."

Son-of-a-bitch.

He didn't think—he just took after the guy. Blood pounded in his head, and he clenched his fists as he raced forward, wanting only to catch the guy and slam his fist right into the thief's ugly face. He wanted to fucking hurt him for scaring her. For stealing from her. For putting his goddamn filthy hands on her.

"Cam! Cam, stop!"

The fear in her voice got through the storm of rage in his head, and he spun around, breathing hard.

"Are you insane! He has a knife. What do you think he'll do if you catch him?"

"He shoved you. He *touched* you."

Her lips parted as if she was going to say more—probably yell at him for being an idiot—but then she drew in a breath and nodded as tears pooled in her eyes.

He sucked in air, then looked around, realizing that he'd followed the guy into one of the side alleys. "He's gone, anyway."

"Look at me. I'm shaking."

"Hey, it's okay now." He put his hands on her shoulders. "He's gone. It's fine. Your phone and credit cards can all be replaced."

She blinked away tears, her voice shaky as she said, "It was only make-up. After Brent told us about him, I put my credit card and driver's license in my back pocket, along with my phone."

"So he got nothing?"

She shook her head. "But I was so afraid he was going to hurt you. Cam, he had a knife. What if he'd stopped? Turned around? He could have c-cut you. He could have k-k-killed you."

He wanted to reassure her. To tell her he was fine. To tell her that the pain and fear in her eyes—fear for him—was the most wonderful, terrifying, humbling thing in the world.

And even though he knew that he might be screwing everything up—even though he knew he should simply hold her and tell her they were both perfectly all right—he did the only thing that he could do.

He leaned in, caught the back of her head, and closed his mouth over hers.

Chapter Five

MINA GASPED as Cam's tongue swept inside her mouth and his body pressed hard against hers. She didn't know if it was lust or adrenaline that pounded through her veins. All she knew was that she wanted this —the taste of him, the feel of him. The strength and safety of his arms.

With heated purpose, his mouth explored hers, his tongue warring with hers, his teeth tugging on her lower lip. It was a kiss that claimed—that demanded surren- der. And she willingly gave herself over to him, wanting nothing more than to get lost in this wild, wicked, and unexpected sensual assault.

Nearby, she could hear the sound of cars rushing down the streets. She could smell the fetid scent of the alley and feel the rough brick abrading her back through the thin cotton of her shirt. But none of that mattered. The only thing she wanted was more—more Cameron, more power, more of the lightning that was crackling around them, making her skin tingle as if electricity was surging through her body, fueled by his touch and her desire.

Gently, he lessened the assault of his kiss, stepping back so that the charged air filled the space between them. At first, she whimpered, wanting to regain that connection, but then he trailed his lips over the soft corner of her mouth, then across her cheek to her ear. His tongue teased her, and she felt the sensation rocket through her, cutting straight to her core and filling her with a liquid heat that made her body throb in silent demand.

"Tell me you like that." Cam's voice was low, powerful, and as it reverberated through her body, she felt more than heard his words.

"Yes." She had to lick her lips because her mouth had gone so dry.

"Me, too," he murmured. "You taste sweet. I want to taste every inch of you."

She whimpered, her imagination conjuring the most wonderful fantasies of his tongue exploring her body. "Cam." The word was soft. A plea, and as if in response, he gently trailed his finger down her body, following the line of her shoulder, her collarbone, then moving on to the swell of her breast.

Her nipples were hard as pebbles, and he teased one lightly through the cotton of her shirt and the thin material of her bra. So lightly that she wanted to scream. To beg him to touch her harder. Wilder. She wanted to get lost in the storm that was ripping through her. More than that, she wanted to get lost in him. His kisses. His touch. His silent demands.

He kept one hand on her breast, but with the other, he continued a slow exploration, leaving her skin light-ning-kissed as he moved lower and lower.

"Yes," she moaned as his hands slid down and found the hem of her tee-shirt. Slowly, he tugged it up, higher and higher until he'd exposed her bra. And when he tugged down her bra cup, then closed his mouth over her breast, she had bite her lip not to scream with pleasure.

The shirt had ridden up her torso, and the feel of the bricks on her now-exposed lower back made some of her sanity return. *They were in an alley. They were in public.*

But she didn't care. Dear God, she really didn't care. She just wanted Cam. This intimacy. This moment.

With his free hand, he fumbled at the button on her jeans, but she pushed his hands away and unfastened them herself. Then she yanked down the zipper with a whispered, "Yes. Oh, please, yes." She craved him, desperate for the feel of him against her, *in* her. His body covering hers, claiming her. *Protecting her.*

He groaned, low in his throat, the sound full of surprise and pleasure. Then his fingers slipped into her panties. She reveled in the connection, closing her eyes and arching her back as his fingers slid down inside her tight jeans, cupping her. "Baby, you're so wet."

"Please." It was the only word she could manage. But with a low, demanding groan, she buried her fingers in his hair, pulling him closer. He took the hint and thrust his fingers inside her.

"Yes," she cried, her mouth hard against his, the sound muffled as he finger-fucked her hard and deep.

"God, Mina, you feel so good."

"Cam," she begged. "I want you inside me."

"Do you have any idea how much I want that, too?"

"Please," she urged, grinding against his hand. She felt lost. Drunk. And she'd only had the one glass of wine, and dammit, she wasn't even scared anymore. She was high on his touch, wild with need. Perfectly sober and drowning in lust and desire and a sexual craving that was so intense it bordered on painful.

Slowly, his fingers moved inside her, and she bit her lip, wriggling against his hand. "You feel so amazing," he said. "I want you, and I'm just drunk enough to take you right here."

"Yes," she said. "Oh, God, yes." She felt her body clench tight around his fingers, then heard his soft sound of surprise and pleasure at the evidence of just how much that idea appealed to her.

He bent his head closer to her ear, his slick fingers stroking her shaved pussy as he slid in and out in a rhythm designed to make her crazed.

"Oh, God, baby," he murmured, his lips caressing the corner of her mouth. "You feel so good it's making me dizzy. I want to turn you around and take you hard against this wall, then get on my knees, spread your legs and taste every inch of you. I want to tease you with my tongue until you beg me to make you come, and I'm just drunk enough to tell you all this out loud."

"Don't just tell me," she whimpered, craving an explosion that seemed just out of reach. "Do it," she begged, so ready for his touch, so desperate to lose herself to him. "Cameron, yes. Now, please."

"I want to," he said, and there was pain in his voice. "You don't know how much I want to."

She looked into his eyes and saw the blue-gray steel of resolve.

"But not now," he whispered, tearing her heart in two. "Not like this."

CAMERON COULDN'T BELIEVE he was actually putting the brakes on. Especially since every cell in his body wanted to turn her around, cup his hands over her breasts, and take her hard. To make her his. To erase the thought of every other guy so that she saw only him. Wanted only him.

And he would.

But not like this. Not in a stinking alley.

She deserved candlelight and silk sheets. Strawberries and champagne. At the very least, she deserved a bed—not to have her back scratched up by rough brick as he buried himself in her. Not to have her remember the rank odor of rotting food instead of the scent of him and the musk of sex.

"Cam. Please."

She stood right in front of him, her mouth mere inches from his, her body boxed in by his palms that were now flat on the brick wall behind her. Her voice was a plea and her eyes—her wonderfully sober eyes—brimmed with a green fire that sparked with blatant, sexual need.

He felt his cock grow harder as his need grew and his resolve faded. He might be a fool who believed he could chase down a thug with a knife, but none of that mattered because this woman—this gorgeous, vibrant, amazing woman—wanted him.

Her hand slid down to cup his balls, and he moaned as liquid fire poured through him. He felt as weak as a kitten and as strong as Hercules, and he leaned forward, burying his face at the crook of her neck as she murmured, "Please. Oh, God, Cam, *please.*"

Yes, he thought. *Oh, hell, yes.* His hands moved to cup her perfect ass. To tug her roughly against him so that he felt the press of her everywhere. Thighs, sex, breasts.

His heart pounded in time with hers, and he knew that if she said his name one more time he really would take her right there—and he also knew that he'd regret it in the morning. Her voice was a plea, an incantation. And he was just tipsy enough to fall under its spell.

With supreme effort, he gathered his resolve. "Not here." Roughly, he pulled away, the motion taking more effort than any regimen of torture he'd suffered in Matthew's gym. For the first time in years he regretted not staying in the South Austin house he and Kiki had inherited from their grandmother. A house where there was privacy. Tons of privacy.

But the house was rented now, and he bunked in a co-op near campus, paid for by his scholarship's housing allowance. But there was no way in hell he was making love to Mina in a ratty twin bed with his suite-mate in the next room jacking off to their moans and the squeak of his bed springs.

"My place." Her voice burned into him, hoarse and urgent.

He thought of Darryl and his room that looked out over the grounds—and Mina's apartment. "Are you sure?"

"Hell, yes."

Thank God.

Tomorrow, Cam would think about the ramifications of sleeping with Mina, the woman he'd craved forever. The woman his best friend watched over like a hawk.

A woman who, Cam had always believed, was so far out of his league he'd have a better shot climbing a ladder to heaven.

But he must have earned his way to salvation, because she'd just invited him through the pearly gates, and for better or worse, there was no way he was saying no.

He stepped back, giving her room to move, but taking her hand as he did, simply because he was unwilling to break the connection. "Are you okay to drive?"

"I'm fine." She licked her lips, looking suddenly unsure. "How about you? Are you okay?"

"I'm not driving."

Her eyes slid away from his. "I mean—"

"I know what you mean," he said, then bent forward to kiss her gently. "And I'm fine. I'm coherent. I'm bubbling over with free will. And," he added as he lifted her hand to his lips and kissed her palm, "I've wanted to do this for about as long as I can remember. The only thing the bourbon's done is give me a jolt of courage."

He could hear the relief in her laughter. "Oh. Well, then thank God for bourbon."

"You got that right."

She fished in her pocket for her keys, and he had to once again admire her foresight in removing everything except her make-up from her purse.

"Let's go. The car's just one block over."

It took only a few minutes to get to her sporty Mercedes, and then only twenty minutes after that to get from downtown to her house on the south side of the river, just off of Redbud Trail. But as far as Cam was concerned, that was twenty minutes too long.

She parked at the end of the drive, as close to the door to her apartment as it was possible to get. And though neither of them spoke about it, Cam knew they were both hurrying to get inside not just to get their hands on each other, but because the faster they got behind closed doors, the less chance there was that Darryl would see them.

Mina fumbled the key in the lock, and then, laughing,

pushed it open and pulled him inside. The door clicked shut behind him, and for a moment, they both just stood there, the hall light shining bright around them, as if they'd been thrust out of a sensual land of shadows and dreams and into the harsh light of an examination room.

"Mina," he said, suddenly unsure of himself, of the situation, of everything.

She swallowed, then took a step back so that she was leaning on the door, her hand resting on the knob as if in silent assurance that she could open it at any time. "I —" She drew a breath and started again. "This is going to sound crazy, but I kind of wish we'd stayed in that horrible alley."

He frowned, trying to parse out her meaning from her words. "Do you want me to go?"

"No," she said, but the word seemed tentative, and he was desperately afraid that what she meant was *yes*. "It's just that I'm thinking about it now. What it was like, I mean."

She spoke so softly that he had to strain to hear her. But then a wild, primal need rippled through his body as his mind finally put the pieces together.

That's what she wanted. That rawness. That fear-induced lust that had overtaken them in that fetid alley and erased their inhibitions. Because Cam knew damn well that if that thief hadn't stolen her purse, she'd have politely driven him home, and he'd have politely said goodnight.

But instead they'd ended up almost fucking in an

alley. They'd crossed a line, goddammit. A line that he'd been dreaming about for most of his life.

And he damn sure didn't intend to turn back now.

He took a single step toward her, but that was enough to put him right in front of her. He said nothing, but reached out and ran his hand along her hairline, his eyes focused on hers. His heart pounded wildly in his chest, but he knew she couldn't tell. He looked calm. He looked in control. And goddammit, he was going to turn that fiction into a reality.

"You have one chance to tell me to go," he said, moving his hand from her face to the wall behind her. The other hand hung by his side, so that she wasn't fully boxed in. "One chance to stop this."

He inched closer. "I'm going to undress you, Mina. I'm going to spread your legs and get on my knees, and I'm going to make you scream my name. And baby, that's just the beginning. So if you want me to go, say so now. Because once I start touching you, I really don't think I can stop."

He held his breath, afraid that she'd seen through his bravado. That now that they were out of the alley she'd realized it was all a big mistake. The world was tilting under him as he gave her a chance to tell him to leave. And when she drew in a breath and her lips moved, the knowledge that she was about to kick him out struck him with the force of a blow.

But then she said nothing. Just pressed her lips together and stared him down. "Good answer," he whispered, then just about melted when her mouth twitched in the tiniest of smiles.

"Arms up," he said, and when she complied, he peeled off her shirt, leaving her in the hallway clad in her jeans and bra.

She released a shaky breath, her teeth on her lower lip. But her eyes were bright with arousal, and he felt a masculine pride in knowing that she wanted him. Wanted the pleasure of surrendering.

Just the thought made him hard, and spurred him on, and soon she stood naked in front of him, her clothes tossed casually toward her couch.

"You're beautiful," he whispered, then watched her skin flush with pleasure.

"I never imagined you like this," she said.

He tilted his head. "So you've imagined me?"

She nodded, and his cock that had gotten hard at the sight of her, now stiffened painfully from the knowledge that he'd played a role in her fantasies.

"If not like this, then how?"

"Sweet," she said, not meeting his eyes.

He laughed. "I can do sweet. Do you want me to?"

He watched her face, the unfocused desire in her eyes. Then he let his eyes trail down to her breasts, her nipples hard, her areolae puckered. She didn't want sweet, and his assumption was proven right when she shook her head and said, "Not tonight."

His stomach flip-flopped with glee. "Next time, then. Tell me what you want tonight."

He already knew, but he wanted her to say it.

"Those things you said in the alley. Or was that the bourbon talking?"

"I don't need bourbon when I'm around you to be buzzed. And I can be sweet when you want me to be. But just so we're clear, Mina, when I imagine you, this is how it is. Because how else could I ever get you if I didn't just take what I want?"

She licked her lips. "Then stop talking and take, already."

He laughed, her playfulness and open desire making him even more turned on. "Yeah," he said, brushing a kiss across her lips. "I think I will."

He hadn't lied when he said he wanted to get on his knees and taste her, but he intended to get there slowly. This beautiful woman was naked in front of him, and he trailed his fingers over her body, exploring and teasing and kissing and tasting, as he worked his way down lower and lower.

He wanted to memorize her skin, her reactions, the places on her body that made her tremble and sigh. And then he wanted to go back to each of them and explore all the decadent possibilities.

Now, he just wanted to revel in the fact that she was right in front of him, naked and open and ready—and that it was him she wanted.

With deliberate slowness, he ran his hands over every inch of her. Exploring, touching, teasing. And only when he was certain he'd committed every curve and every freckle to memory did he ease down onto his knees as he pressed gentle kisses from her cleavage to her navel, and then lower still.

She was so damn wet, and she tasted sweet and earthy and feminine. He teased her clit with the tip of his tongue, and she surprised him by grabbing his hair as her whole body shook. He smiled, realizing she was closer than he'd thought, and he used his hands to gently spread her thighs, and as she knotted her fingers in his hair, he sucked and teased and licked and tasted as he reveled in the scent and taste of her.

He didn't let her come, though, and when he slowly kissed his way up her body she begged him to rectify that little oversight.

"You promised to make me come," she said, when he only held out his hand to lead her to the bedroom.

"I promised to make you scream. And I did."

Her eyes narrowed, and she tossed a couple of not so nice names in his direction. But it was true. She'd screamed his name. Screamed that she was close.

And now she was even closer. Now when he took her in the bed, he knew that she'd explode.

That's where they were going, of course. Because, frankly, Cameron couldn't stand waiting another second to be inside her. And as he walked, he unbuttoned his shirt and slipped out of his shoes so that once they reached the bedroom it would be easier to get naked.

Easier still with Mina's eager fingers helping undress him.

When he was naked, she slowly looked him up and down, subjecting him to the same inspection through which he'd put her. She lingered at his cock, then raised her eyes to his. "You'll do," she said, making him laugh.

"Do you have a condom."

"Only one in my wallet," he said. "I wasn't anticipating tonight."

"That's okay. I'm a girl who likes to be prepared. There's more if we need them."

He pulled her close and cupped her ass. "I think we'll need them," he said, and she nodded, laughing.

"On the bed," he said, but this time she shook her head. "My turn to do a little exploring," she said, pointing toward the bed and ordering him to stretch out. It was, frankly, a command he wasn't about to disobey

He laid down, and she got on top of him, straddling him at the waist and sitting just low enough that her ass rubbed against his cock. "Thought I'd torment you a little," she said, wriggling.

"If this is your idea of torment, I'll take it."

She kissed him, then winked, then laid her body on top of his, her heat coiling through him and firing his senses. "I like your chest," she murmured, kissing it lightly, then lifting her head to meet his eyes. "Keep working out."

"Yes, ma'am."

"And your earring," she added, sliding up his body so that she could suck on his earlobe and the small gold stud he'd worn since he and Darryl got drunk freshman year. "Darryl let his piercing close up, but I'm glad you kept it. It's sexy."

She trailed her finger to his mouth. "And these lips. I

like them, especially," she said, and kissed him soft and deep, then surprised him by sucking hard on his lower lip. So hard he felt the intensity of it all the way in his cock.

"Christ, Mina," he groaned when she did it again. "You're going to make me come without even trying."

"Oh, I'm trying," she said, then laughed. "Want to watch me try harder?" She eased down him, peering up coyly before wrapping her hand around his cock and then running her tongue over the tip.

He closed his eyes, arching his head back and surrendering to the building intensity that she was wreaking within him. His body seeming to reduce to nothing but his cock and her mouth, and it was so fucking incredible the way the explosion built, coming closer and closer and—

"*Mina.*"

It took all of his strength, but he pulled away, then flipped her over so that it was his turn to straddle her. "Inside you," he said, so desperate to have her that he could barely utter the words.

She nodded, her face bright with desire as she pulled her knees up, giving herself to him. "Yes. God, yes."

He didn't waste any time. He was hard as steel and almost came simply from looking at her pussy, all pink and wet and ready for him. "It'll be fast," he said, hurrying to slide on a condom before thrusting deep inside her. "I can't go slow."

"Fast is good," she said, moving in time with his thrusts. "Fast is great."

The both fell silent then, their bodies now doing all the talking as he claimed her. As he sank deep inside her. As he made her his.

And when he felt her core tighten around his cock, he couldn't hold back any longer. "Come with me," he demanded, and she arched up crying out, "Yes, yes," as she went over, her climax coming so hard and so intense that she milked him dry, and he collapsed, spent, on the bed beside her, his body little more than a well-satisfied shell.

She curled up next to him, practically purring, and he draped and arm over her waist, letting the warmth of their joined bodies curl through them. He felt amazing —and at the same time, a little surreal.

This was Mina. Naked and satisfied in his arms.

The woman he'd wanted forever.

The girl who was his best friend's sister.

The sudden reality hit him like a splash of cold water. *He'd slept with Mina.* With the "little" sister that Darryl had looked out for his whole life.

He drew in a breath, not entirely sure how to handle that particular truth. But one course of action came to mind and he started to sit up.

"Hey," she protested, pulling him back. "What are you doing?"

"I should probably go," he said, reluctantly pulling away from her to sit on the side of the bed.

"Go?"

He squinted at the floor searching for his pants, then looked back at her over his shoulder. "It's ridiculously late. Do you think I should walk down to the street? If I call for a ride share and it comes up the drive, Darryl might wake up and notice. And I don't think he—"

"Cam." She propped herself up on her elbow, the sheet falling away to reveal one perfect breast as she said his name.

"Mina, I—"

She reached out, then rested her hand gently over his. "Stay," she said. "I want to do that again."

And so he did.

Chapter Six

MINA CAME AWAKE SLOWLY, her fuzzy mind trying to make sense of all the wonderful sensations. The sunlight tickling her nose as it streamed in through the east-facing window. The equally enticing heat of Cam's breath against the back of her neck. The warmth of his skin as he spooned against her.

And, most interesting of all, the decadent promise of his erection pressing insistently against her bare ass.

Smiling to herself, she wiggled a bit, not sure if he was awake or simply aroused in his sleep. The latter wouldn't surprise her. If he was anything like her, his night had been filled with dreams that were at least as erotic as the reality they'd shared before falling asleep. And as hard as he was, she knew that she was equally wet.

And, dammit, she really hoped that he was awake.

"Careful," he murmured, his voice gravelly with

sleep. "Do that again and you'll be hard-pressed to get me out of here this morning."

His words filled her with delight, and she pressed her face against the pillow to stifle her laugher as she wriggled against him again.

"Now you've done it," he said, and any thoughts of waking up slowly and lazily evaporated as he pulled her roughly over, then straddled her.

"Don't even try to escape," he teased. "You're totally under my control."

"You've got that right," she said, happily surrendering as he slid down, so that he was partially under the sheet with her. He lowered his mouth to her breast and sucked, sending spirals of pleasure curling through her.

And then, right when she thought the sensation couldn't be any more tantalizing, he grazed his teeth against her nipple, just enough that she wasn't sure if it hurt … or felt absolutely amazing.

"You like that," he said as she squirmed beneath him, her body craving more.

"I like everything you do to me," she said honestly.

"Good, because there's a whole world of everything out there for us to explore." As if to illustrate the point, he moved down lower and lower, so that he was nestled between her legs. The sheet moved with him, leaving him exposed from the waist up. But, sadly, his cute ass was completely covered.

She realized soon enough that it didn't matter how cute his butt was, because the things he was doing to her down there were so amazing that she couldn't concentrate on her own sensations, much less his ass.

He'd kept one hand on her breast, and now he rolled her nipple tight between his fingers. That alone could send her right over the edge. But he didn't stop there. He'd nestled his shoulders between her inner thighs, and his mouth covered her sex, his tongue dancing over her clit, then dipping inside her folds. And the combination of nipple play and the stimulation on her clit was enough to make her positively lose her mind.

So much, that she was writhing shamelessly on the bed, her hips gyrating in a way that made his five o'clock shadow rub enticingly over her sex. And her own fingers on her other nipple mimicked the motions he was so expertly executing.

She was in a wild haze, a rising storm of passion, and with each thrust of her hips, his tongue and fingers took her higher. It was as if they were dancing, moving in a pattern so well-known it was almost instinctual. And when he used his free hand to thrust two fingers deep inside her, she felt a spiderweb of electricity shoot out from her core to escape through her fingers and toes.

So close … she was so damn close.

"Again," she begged, then repeated the demand, her voice breaking as his mouth closed over her sex. Her lips parted, her head tilting back as she moaned with pleasure—and then squealed with surprise as her bedroom door burst open.

"Christ, Darryl! What the hell!" Even as she yelled

at her brother, she'd yanked the sheet up around her chin, completely covering Cam, who'd had enough of his wits about him to tug his hand down under at the same time. His face, though, was still between her legs, and the feel of his breath against her tender—and aroused—sex was more than a little distracting.

"You said come in!" To his credit, he looked embarrassed.

"I said *again*, you moron. Do you want to get the hell out of here?"

He glanced at the bulge under the sheet, his eyes narrowing. He knew that she had a few guy friends that she slept with but didn't actually date. Like Jeff, for example. She also knew he disapproved.

"Do you mind?" she snapped.

He shook his head as if to clear it. "Sorry—I just— you said you had a run this morning. It never occurred to me you'd brought anyone home."

Fuck. The 5K. She'd completely forgotten. She'd signed up with her friend, Taylor, and she made a mental note to call and explain.

"Can we talk about my physical fitness later? I'm kind of in the middle of something."

"Um, yeah. Sure. No problem. I just wanted to know what time to tell Zach to show up for the party tonight."

Between her legs, she felt Cam stiffen, and she forced herself not to yell at her brother that she wasn't interested in a fix-up or a relationship or an arranged marriage or any of the ridiculous scenarios that were bouncing around in her brother's head. But instead, all she said was, "Six. You can tell him that your not-really-a-surprise party is at six. Now get the hell out of here."

He actually laughed—bastard—then started to head out. "I'm going to brunch with the judge," he reminded her. "If you and your boy toy decide to frolic naked in the pool, just remember we have security cameras."

She grabbed Mr. Meow, the stuffed cat she'd had since infancy, off her bookshelf-style headboard and hurled it at him. But he was already gone, and the poor cat smacked into the now-closed door.

Beneath the sheets, she felt Cam relax before he slowly emerged. She scooted over so that he could share the pillow, then grabbed hold of his hand as they both exhaled loudly.

"Holy fuck," he said, and she thought that summed the situation up nicely.

They both stared at the ceiling, just breathing, for at least five long minutes. Then Cam rolled over and propped himself up on his elbow. With his free hand, he traced random patterns on her belly, making her skin tighten as a new electricity started to zing through her. Because, apparently, she hadn't yet had enough of him. Who would have thought that the Cam who'd tormented her as a kid would be such a tender lover?

No, she corrected. *Not tender*. He was, yes. But there was a roughness, too. An edginess. He'd *claimed* her, no other way to describe it. And dear God, she'd surrendered completely. Willingly.

She liked men who took charge—that much she

knew. But she'd never looked at Cam and seen that side of him. He was so sweet. So nice. Smart and funny and serious about his studies.

All qualities she admired. After all, she worked hard at school and on her job, and she'd locked onto her career path with laser-like focus. She recognized commitment when she saw it. Admired it, too.

But somehow, she'd never seen that side of Cam before.

Had she not been looking? Or had he always been hidden by Darryl's shadow?

"Thinking deep thoughts?" he asked, sliding his hand down along the curve of her waist to rest on her hip. "Or trying not to think about Darryl's surprise appearance."

"Both," she said. "And neither."

He nipped at her earlobe, making her squeal. "I like a woman who speaks in riddles."

"Actually, I was thinking about you."

"Yeah?" He lifted his head, his expression wary, but pleased. "What were you thinking?"

"That you surprised me, Cameron Reed."

"Did I? I bet I can do it again."

"What? Surprise me? I sincerely doubt it."

He didn't answer. Instead, he slid his hand between her thighs, then roughly thrust two fingers deep inside her. "Surprise," he whispered.

CAM SWALLOWED A MOAN, his cock growing hard again as his fingers explored her slick heat. Would he ever get enough of this woman?

Honestly, he really didn't think so. And despite the mortification factor from Darryl walking in on them—and almost seeing way more than Cam would ever be inclined to share with his best friend—he was pretty much floating on cloud nine at the moment.

"Oh, God, Cam." She arched up, grinding against his hand as if she, too, couldn't get her fill. "What are you trying to do to me?"

His fingers continued their merciless tease. "Right now? I'm just trying to make you come. Why? Do you think I should be doing more

"Honestly? I think you're doing exactly the right amount. Don't stop, okay?"

He wouldn't dream of it, and he touched and teased until she exploded once again in his arms, and a warm wave of satisfaction crested inside him from the simple knowledge that he'd brought her to such dizzying heights.

"We have to stop," she murmured, stretching as the last shudders of the orgasm fizzled away. She rolled over, then smiled as she eased on top and nestled her head under his chin, her breasts firm and warm against his chest. "I came so hard, I'm not even sure if all the pieces of me are put back together right."

He ran his hands over her shoulder blades, then down her back, then over the curve of her ass. "You feel pretty well-put together to me."

"Mmm," she said, her face pressed to his skin. "I think I know what's happened to us," she said.

"You mean more than mind-blowing passion?"

"That's a result," she said. "I know the cause."

He stroked her back, his fingers tracing lazily over her bare skin. "Okay," he said. "Enlighten me."

"We flipped a switch," she said. And when he didn't respond, she added, "It's as if you and I were stumbling around in a dark room. And then one day, one of us finds a light switch. Suddenly, we see each other. It was all there before, we just missed it."

"I never did," he admitted. "I've wanted this since we were kids."

She propped herself up. "*This*? Because that makes you a seriously precocious little kid."

"Back then I mostly wanted to share your lemonade, sit by you in our fort, and try to get a peek when you changed into your swimsuit behind a towel."

"Perv."

"How about you? Any lingering child fantasies with me in the starring role?"

Her cute little nose wrinkled. "Sorry, no."

"And now?"

Her laughter was like the trill of bells. "Now? Oh, now there are tons of fantasies. Buckets of fantasies."

"Then I guess you're right. You flipped a switch."

She kissed him gently. "Yeah," she said, her voice tender. "I guess I did."

"And is that a good thing?"

"Insecure much?"

"Hell, no."

She laughed. "Glad to hear it. And that switch? A very, very good thing."

"How about those fantasies?"

She closed her eyes and sighed, her teeth scraping over her lower lip. "Those are good, too."

"Tell me," he demanded, but she just smiled and shook her head.

"Sorry, mister. You'll have to wait. We need to get moving. I've got a party to pull together."

"I can help you."

For a second, she hesitated. Then she propped herself up, her elbows digging painfully into his gut. Not that he intended to complain. "That's okay," she said. "I can manage."

Alarm bells didn't exactly clang in his head, but they were definitely starting to *ding* a bit. "You're sure? I don't mind?"

"No, seriously. It's fine. You must have stuff to do on a Saturday." As she sat up, she held the sheet over her breasts and the *dinging* ratcheted up a notch. "I should probably go take a shower."

He reached for her hand. "Hold up a sec. What about tonight."

She blinked. "Tonight?"

"The party," he said. "This guy Zach's coming. Shouldn't we—"

"What?" The word came out sharp, cutting him off, and he couldn't help but fear that he heard a note of panic in her voice.

He drew a breath, telling himself to be calm. That any weirdness he was picking up on was probably coming from him. From the down-rush of adrenaline he was experience after having every fantasy in his life fulfilled over one glorious night. Of course he was going to be on edge. Of course, he was expecting her to yank the carpet out from under him.

"It's only that I think we should tell Darryl."

For a second, she looked confused. Then her eyes went wide. "Oh! You mean about this." She indicated the two of them. "About us?"

"Well, yeah. I mean, if he's trying to set you up with—"

She waved her hand, dismissing the words. "Believe me. I can already tell I'm not interested in Zach. And I doubt he'd be interested in me."

"Well, then—"

"But say something to Darryl?" Her voice rose with incredulity. "Really bad idea."

He sat up in bed, and since she had the sheet, he used the quilt to cover himself. Because suddenly, he felt the need to be covered. "Why?"

"Well, think about it. This is fun—hell, it's been amazing. And I don't know about you, but I'm totally hoping we do it again."

Thank God.

"Yeah," he said, forcing his voice to stay level and even. "Me, too."

"But what happens later? I mean, say around Christmas time when we've both moved on but we're all together for the holidays. If Darryl knows what his sister and best friend did during the summer, it's totally awkward. But if he doesn't know…"

She lifted her shoulder in a shrug as her voice trailed off.

He stared. He just freaking stared.

"Cam? That makes sense, right?"

And that's when he realized that Mina Silver was a magician. Because somehow, without him even realizing it, she'd pulled that damn carpet right out from under him.

Chapter Seven

"I CAN'T BELIEVE you stood us up," Taylor D'Angelo said as she perched on one of the stools in front of the breakfast bar, her dark brown hair pulled back into a long ponytail. "What was it you'd said? Nothing's better for your ass than running and squats?"

"Well, it's true." Mina passed Taylor a water bottle, and then handed a second one to Megan, whose fair skin still bloomed pink with exertion.

"The hell it is," Taylor retorted, sliding off the bar stool, then positioning herself so that her rear end was aimed at the kitchen. She looked over her shoulder to Mina. "Still flat as a pancake. Whereas yours is all perky. And not because of running, I might add. No, your ass was treated to a booty call workout."

Beside her, Megan almost choked on her water.

"Well, it's true," Taylor said. "How much do you want to bet she stood us up because she was lost in post-coital bliss?"

"Not disagreeing. I was just thinking about the possibilities of a booty call exercise video."

As Taylor and Megan laughed, Mina rolled her eyes. "Are you two about done yet?"

Taylor's mouth curved into a thoughtful frown. "I think so. How about you?"

Megan shrugged. "Completely done."

"Good, because—"

"Actually, I take it back," Taylor said. "I'm not done."

Mina let out a low, suffering groan, then pretended to bang her head on the kitchen wall. The banging was mimed. But the suffering was real. Because Mina knew damn well that once Taylor got something in her head, she didn't let it go easily.

She'd known Taylor since high school, although they'd really only become close in college after they kept ending up in the same classes during undergrad. Now, Taylor was a grad student in the drama department and was also stage managing the calendar contest for The Fix on Sixth, making sure the stage was properly set, the microphones were working, the guys all knew what to do, and all the other details that freed up Jenna—the partner at The Fix who was overseeing the contest—to focus on the big picture.

Mina didn't know Megan nearly as well, though she liked the recent transplant from LA.

A make-up artist, Megan had met Taylor when Megan had done the pre-photoshoot makeup for one of their mutual friends. Megan had also become close with

Mina's old boss, Griffin, although Mina still didn't know if Megan and Griff were dating or just friends.

Either way, Mina liked Megan a lot, and when Taylor suggested that Megan join them on the fun run, Mina had easily agreed.

Of course, completely forgetting about the race probably wasn't the best way to make a good impression on her new friend…

"Come on, Taylor," Mina said now, before Taylor could make that very point. Or, possibly, a thousand more points. "I said I was sorry." She looked at Megan. "And I really am sorry."

Megan held up the now-empty water bottle. "It's no big deal, really. It's not like we were going to have scintillating conversation as we ran. I was doing good to draw air, actually."

Taylor narrowed her pretty brown eyes in Megan's direction. "You're too damn nice. And as for you," she added, turning her attention to Mina, "I have just one word—*who?*"

"Who?" Mina repeated.

"Yes. Duh. *Who.* Who was more important than running solidarity? Please tell me it wasn't Jeff. He's nice enough, but that's not going anywhere."

"Jeff?" Megan asked.

"This guy. They're not dating, but…" She twirled her finger in the air. "You know."

"It's not a big deal," Mina said, then opened the pantry door to inspect the contents. "Jeff and I are just—"

"Friends with benefits?" Taylor put in.

"As a matter of fact, yes. What's wrong with that?" She knew she sounded testy, and she honestly wasn't sure why. The thing with Jeff *wasn't* a big deal because she didn't want it to be.

"Nothing wrong at all," Taylor said, and from her appeasing tone, Mina knew that her friend had caught the edge in Mina's voice.

"At any rate, it wasn't Jeff," she said, then added *salsa* to the grocery list she was making for tonight's party. It was going to be small—just a dozen or so of Darryl's friends—but she still wanted to be sure there was enough food and alcohol.

"Tossed him aside, have you?" Taylor pressed the back of her hand to her forehead as if in a swoon, and Megan immediately laughed.

"Don't be melodramatic," Mina said. But even as she spoke the words, she knew that Taylor had hit on the truth. Jeff was of the past. And Cameron—well, she hoped he was of the present. But she was afraid they'd gone off the rails. Worse, she was afraid she'd steered them that direction.

All she'd wanted to do was not shine a spotlight on the two of them. And even though he'd finally told her that he understood her point, there'd been a look in his eyes that had made her stomach twist with regret.

"Boy, those people who design dating apps must love you," Taylor said. "You're like the poster child."

"That is so not true," Mina protested, Taylor's completely unfair accusation pulling her from her thoughts. "I don't have a little black book, and I don't have a different guy on speed dial every night."

"No, you don't. You're right. But we've been friends for a long time, and I've watched you push away guys who wanted to get serious."

"That's the point," Mina said. "The *guys* wanted to get serious. Not me. Not now. I mean, someday, sure. But I don't have time for distractions."

Even as she spoke, she thought of Cam's slightly crooked grin, of his commanding manner and firm voice. Of all the tantalizing things he'd whispered to her, and then the way his fingers and lips and cock had followed through with such delectable efficiency. Maybe she didn't have time for the distraction, but she'd damn sure enjoyed it.

"I get that," Megan said. "It's hard to focus on your business if you're sidetracked by romance."

"Exactly," Mina said. "Why would I work so hard at school and my internships and all my various projects over the years if I wasn't completely committed to my career? And how can I be *completely* committed to getting my career off the ground if I'm supposed to be committed to a relationship, too? Later, yeah. But right now is critical."

Surely Cam felt the same way? He'd been killing himself to get through two masters programs, and now that he'd been accepted into a Ph.D. program he was going to be even more busy.

Taylor actually threw up her hands. "Okay. Fine. You win."

"Thank you." She exhaled loudly, feeling smug. "I wish you could tell that to Darryl. He's bringing some guy to the party tonight hoping that we'll hit it off." She made a face. "He thinks that since Zach is going into the entertainment industry it'll be a match made in heaven."

"Well, wouldn't it?" Megan asked. "If he's in your business, then it's not really a distraction, is it? More like a perk."

Mina shrugged. "Maybe." Hell, maybe she was resisting Zach because he was Darryl's set up. Maybe the guy really was great.

Maybe.

But even if he was, Mina knew it wouldn't matter. Yesterday, she might have managed to peel her eyes open to really give the guy a look. But today…

Well, today, all she could see was Cam's face. All she could think about was the brush of his fingers over her skin and the way he'd made her feel. Not sex. And not even just fun, but fun and warmth and wildness and need all rolled into one.

She didn't want a relationship—really she didn't.

But she couldn't deny that she craved him. And she hoped like hell that when he'd walked out of her apartment that morning, he hadn't intended it to be forever.

She avoided Taylor and Megan's question about whom she'd slept with, then finally pushed them out the door with the excuse that she had to get to the store, and that she'd see both of them that night since Taylor was coming with Amanda, a mutual friend, and Megan was coming with Griffin.

"I can't ask him, since I interned for him, but are you and Griffin dating?" Mina asked as she walked her friends to Taylor's car.

Megan shook her head. "I won't deny that there was a spark when we first met—or, at least, I thought so. But no."

"I'm sorry."

"Don't be. Honestly, it wouldn't have lasted, and I'm not sure we would have become friends with that kind of history hanging between us."

Mina swallowed, thinking of Cameron. Had they screwed up? Was that unreadable expression she'd seen on his face advance warning of goodbye?

"He's the best," Megan said, unaware of Mina's spiraling thoughts. "But he's got a lot to overcome, and it gets in the way. I hope he finds someone, but I think she's going to have to be a fighter to get through his thick skin. And I don't mean the scars," she added.

"I hear you." Griffin had been horribly injured in a fire when he was a kid, and his face and one side of his body were still messed up. She knew he was in some sort of experimental drug trial, but that wasn't going to magically erase the scars or give the wounded little boy who lived inside the man a shot of confidence.

Once Taylor and Megan were gone, Mina dove into getting the house ready and the food delivered. The food was the easiest, since all she had to do was call the store and ask her father's assistant to send a runner over with everything on the list. For that matter, the house was easy, too. Her father had a housekeeper who came every other day whether the house needed it or not. She'd cleaned and dusted just yesterday, which meant that all Mina had to do was put away the groceries when they arrived, pretty up the party trays, bring up a few bottles of wine from the cellar, and hang the *Congratulations* banner over the big bay window.

And, of course, she had to make the cake. Duncan Hines yellow cake mix with chocolate Betty Crocker frosting. Simple—although considering her lack of skill at frosting, it would still be messy—but it was both of their favorites, and no way was she throwing her brother any type of party without making him a cake.

"Smell's amazing," Darryl said, coming into the kitchen and dropping his keys into the bowl on the breakfast table.

"Only the best for my big brother." She'd just finished frosting the cake, and she passed him the canister. "In case you didn't get enough food at your brunch."

"More than enough," he said. "But there's always room for frosting." He demonstrated by using his finger to scoop up a glob. "So my surprise is at six?"

"I'm not even calling it a surprise party anymore. Now it's an ingrate party."

He waved a chocolate-covered finger at her. "Not ungrateful. Just not surprised."

"Yes, six." She'd deliberately made the party early so that folks realized that it was an understated gathering. They could come by, hang out, and still keep all their Saturday night plans. Plus, even though Mina hadn't invited many folks from The Fix since that was her world and not Darryl's, there were a few crossovers. And since it was a Saturday night, Mina hadn't wanted to pull them away from the busiest hours.

She and Darryl had gone to high school with Tiffany Russell, one of the waitresses, so she was a given. And Jenna and Reece were coming, too. Over Christmas break, Darryl and Reece had spent a full evening talking about restoring old cars—a hobby that Darryl loved but never had time for. It wasn't a huge connection, but the guys had hit it off, and Mina liked both Reece and Jenna.

And, of course, Cam.

But she didn't linger on the thought of him, because the second he'd sidled into her psyche, she'd felt that warm twitchiness, that soft craving.

Cam was a problem she wouldn't be able to solve until she put on her big girl panties and had a talk with him. In the meantime, he lingered in her thoughts for the rest of the day, rising to the surface at inopportune times, like when she was showering, the sudden memory of him so intense that her skin prickled and she felt herself go soft with desire.

She'd barely pulled herself together when the party started—and then there he was again, walking in the door with Tiffany on his arm. Cam looked so casually sexy in jeans and a Henley that Mina had to fight the urge to touch him. And Tiffany looked far too cute in a pink sundress and flats, her wavy hair clipped up so that tendrils framed her round face. *Bitch*, Mina thought, but immediately felt guilty. Until that moment, she'd always liked Tiffany.

When Mina realized she'd been standing silently in front of them, she forced a wide, hostess smile. "Sorry, I'm still running over my party list in my head. It's so great to see you." She pulled Tiffany into a hug. "Thanks for coming. And you, too, of course," she added to Cam. "But he was a given," she added to Tiffany. "Years of being attached to Darryl's hip."

"I remember," Tiffany said. "Well, not during school —you went somewhere south, right?" she asked Cam, who nodded. "But whenever I saw you guys during the summer at the mall or Barton Springs you were always together."

"We've been tight for years," Cam said, then held his arms out to Mina. "What? I'm practically a member of the family. I don't get a hug, too?"

She rolled her eyes. "Of course you do," she said, then slid into his embrace. She'd expected it to be a quick, perfunctory hug. It wasn't. He pulled her close, so that their bodies were pressed tight together. One of his hands rested on her back, the other lightly squeezed her ass. And when she started to pull away, his voice purred low and commanding against her ear. "You were right," he said, and she knew that he felt her shiver.

Then he pulled back, offered Tiffany his arm, and led her into the party, leaving Mina standing stupidly in the doorway wondering what the hell he'd meant by that.

"SHE KEEPS WATCHING YOU," Tiffany said. "What did you say to her?"

Cam and Tiffany were tucked into a corner of the living room. Tiffany was leaning against the edge of a bookcase, and he was standing in front of her, close enough that it looked intimate. "I only told her she was right."

"About what?" Tiffany asked.

"That's what she's going to be wondering." He reached forward and untangled a strand of hair from her hoop earring. Innocent enough, but it would undoubtedly look intimate to anyone paying attention.

And, yes, he knew he was being an ass, but he didn't care. He had a point to make, and setting the stage with Tiffany was the fastest way he could think of to do it.

"I can't believe you talked me into this," she said.

"Into what? All you're doing is coming with me to my best friend's welcome back party. We came together. That's it."

She smirked. "Fine, don't tell me. It's not like I told you about my crush on Eric. Which, by the way, I totally expect you to keep secret."

"Don't you trust me?" They'd started working at The Fix the same week, and then learned that they shared three classes. There'd never been any sexual attraction between them, but Cam and Tiff had become fast friends.

"Don't *you* trust *me?*" she countered.

"Fine. We slept together."

Tiffany stared at him like he was an idiot. "Well, duh. Nobody goes through these kinds of machinations if sex isn't at stake."

He couldn't help it, he burst out laughing. "Let's mingle, and I'll give you the full scoop."

They walked, and he did, making sure to talk when they wouldn't be overheard. The bottom line was that Mina's speech in bed had been one serious kick in the heart, not to mention parts further south. He understood not wanting to tell Darryl—hell, he'd spent years not making a move on Mina because of her brother—but her talk about it inevitably ending had twisted him up way more than it probably should. So much so that he'd gone home, stood in the shower until the water ran cold, and replayed the conversation over and over and over, trying to figure out what about it had made him feel like such a damn loser.

It wasn't the way she'd reacted to him, that was for sure. She'd said she wanted him, and everything they'd done together had been evidence that she'd meant it.

She'd also dismissed the very idea of Zach, which had definitely made him happy.

She'd even suggested that they'd have a reasonably long run. After all, it was only early June, and she'd mentioned Christmas.

That, however, was the problem.

"A timeline," Tiffany said, and he shrugged. "She saw the end before you two had even begun."

"You sound like a psychology major," he said, which made her laugh because, of course, she was.

They were by the table with all the alcohol, and he poured her a glass of wine as his eyes searched the living room and the connecting patio. The doors were open, and guests were mingling inside and by the pool. He saw Darryl talking to Nolan and waved, but his gaze didn't linger until he finally found Mina. She was standing by the pool chatting with Easton, a local lawyer who was a regular at The Fix and, Cam knew, did work for her father's company.

As if she'd felt his gaze on her, she looked up, her eyes finding him immediately. He saw a flash of heat in her eyes, then her brow furrow as if in question.

He looked away, his heart pounding, and offered the wine to Tiffany.

"She says she doesn't do commitment, and I can live with that."

"You can?"

"In a way." He'd thought about it a lot. He wanted to try and start something with her; he knew that. He wanted to go slow and see what grew. To twine their lives together even more than they already were and see if they ended up being a fit.

They already had so much in common. Both focused on their educations and careers. Both with successful siblings. Both trying to prove that they could make it on their own. Him, despite growing up with no money and no parents. Her, despite a physical frailty and a father and brother who couldn't seem to believe that she'd left those weaknesses behind.

He saw all that with the same clarity that he saw a story from the past play out in his mind as he pored over ancient documents. But those same documents also told him that sometimes the end was inevitable. The pieces on the chess board set in a way that no other outcome was fathomable.

And with Mina, she always set the board up for failure.

"But that's not anything you can change," Tiffany said after he'd laid it all out for her.

"No, but Mina can." He nodded across the room to where Jenna stood, her back to Reece's chest, their arms entwined. Gently, Reece tilted his head and pressed a kiss to Jenna's hair. "They were friends," he said. "Now look at them."

"Jenna's pregnant, you know," Tiffany said.

He'd suspected as much; she'd stopped drinking alcohol during her off hours. "Did she tell you?"

"She glows. Plus the water."

"They fit. And you can damn well believe neither one of them went in thinking that it would be over by Christmas. Because they both wanted the other one too bad."

Tiffany turned away from Jenna and Reece to look up at him, her eyes wide. "You devil," she said. "You're making her jealous."

"Nah," he said. "I just want her to notice. I just want her to *want*. Not the fling. *Me*. At the very least, that might get us past Christmas and all the way to Valentine's Day."

He thought the comment would make her laugh, but instead, she just looked thoughtful. Then she stepped closer, until she was mere inches from him. She set her wine aside, then took his and put it down, too. "Don't even look her way," she whispered. "But I think now would be a very good time for us to go."

Chapter Eight

"ARE YOU LOOKING FOR MY DADDY?"

Mina turned away from Brent's living room window to find Faith's big blue eyes staring back at her. "Oh, no honey. Your daddy's working all day. I was looking for a friend."

"Aunt Jenna and Uncle Reece?" the five year old asked, bouncing in her footie pajamas.

"No, sweetie. I think they're at work with your daddy. I was looking out for my friend Cameron. You know Cam, right? He works with your dad? And he'd said he was going to help me sit with you."

Faith clapped her hands. "He plays fort with me."

Despite her melancholy, Mina couldn't suppress her smile. She had vivid memories of Cam engineering all sorts of forts in the vacant lot down the street from where he'd lived with his grandmother and sister, Kiki. He'd spend hours poring over books filled with pictures of medieval castles and forts, and then he'd try to recreate them out of abandoned building material, discarded furniture, and soggy cardboard boxes.

Once the forts were up, he and Darryl would round up the neighborhood kids, and Cam would assign all their parts. Never did the two opposing sides just attack; no, for Cam, their neighborhood battles rose to the level of historical re-enactment.

She bit back a smile, remembering what a nerd he'd been. Still was, she supposed. But a damn sexy one.

With a heavy heart, she reached down for Faith's hand. "I don't think he's coming," she said. "Come on. Let's get you changed. And then maybe we can go do something. What do you think? Want to go on an adventure?"

"Puppies?" Faith asked, jumping up and down. And since Brent had forewarned her that one of Faith's favorite places was the nearby Brentwood Neighborhood Park because so many of the locals brought their dogs out to play, Mina nodded in agreement.

"We'll get changed and go see if there are any puppies, and then maybe we can get some lunch, okay?" It was already after ten, but Faith had been watching cartoons in her PJs when Mina arrived. Now, the little girl rushed off to find some clothes, and Mina lingered more slowly behind, feeling lonely and melancholy.

She'd known she'd screwed up with Cam the second she'd seen his face in bed yesterday morning. That stupid, foolish moment when she'd pretty much told him that it would be over by Christmas.

All she'd wanted was to be clear. She liked him—

and God knew she'd liked sleeping with him—but she wasn't ready to get serious. Not with him. Not with anyone.

But that didn't mean they couldn't have fun.

Except apparently it did, because it hadn't taken him any time at all to switch his attention away from her and over to Tiffany.

And to think she actually *liked* Tiffany.

Or she had once upon a time. Now she was thinking that Tiff fell into the category of raging bitch.

Which wasn't fair, she knew, but at the moment Mina didn't care.

But, honestly, he couldn't wait a few days to date someone else? Especially when he'd offered to help her babysit, and now not only was he blowing her off, but he was probably off blowing another woman?

Her chest tightened with the thought, and she grabbed her phone, then started to pull up his contact information, because right then the only thing she really wanted to do was give him a piece of her mind.

She hit the button, the call connected, rang once, and then her sanity returned. *What the hell was she doing?*

She scrambled to end the call, but before she could manage, she heard his voice.

"Mina?"

"You're a jerk."

"Nah, I'm a great guy. Everybody says so."

"I don't. You're supposed to be helping me babysit. You went on and on about how I didn't know what I was doing, and you have tons of experience, and I'd be an idiot to try to watch over Faith without you around."

There was a beat, and then he said, "Well, that's pretty much how I remember our conversation."

"You stood me up," she said. "And you brought Tiffany to Darryl's party." *Damn.* That just slipped out.

"I did. But you invited her."

"Obviously poor judgment on my part."

"Why? I thought you guys were friends."

"Friends don't swoop in on guys that their friends are sleeping with." She said the last in a whisper as she walked down the hall to check on Faith, who was sitting on her bed playing with her stuffed animals.

"You mean me?" he asked as Mina backed out, not wanting to disturb the little girl.

"No, I mean Santa Claus. Of course I mean you."

"And, ah, how was Tiffany supposed to know that we'd slept together? I thought it was a secret. When you said we couldn't tell Darryl, that pretty much meant we couldn't tell anyone, right? Certainly not someone like Tiffany who's his friend."

She returned to the living room, then paced from the front door to the kitchen. "You know what, you're right. Tiffany's fine. She's a goddess. A model of purity and sweetness. She's practically Emily Post. *You're* the asshole."

"I'm pretty sure that's where we started this conversation. Only then I was a jerk. What have I done in the last two minutes to make my stature drop to asshole?"

"You know what—forget it. I can handle a five-year-old. And as for you and Tiffany, you just have a grand old time, okay?"

"Mina."

"I'll see you at The Fix, I'm sure."

"Mina."

"I need to go check on Faith."

"*Mina.*"

"*What?*"

"Open the front door."

She froze, the door just inches away. "What did you say?"

This time when he answered, his voice was gentle. "Open the front door."

She did, and when she saw him leaning against the porch railing, such a wave of relief washed over her that she had to hold onto the doorframe to steady herself. "You came to babysit."

He took a step toward her. "I came for you."

"Oh."

"You want to go inside? Or should I kiss you here on the front porch where anyone can see?"

Her stomach dropped, but the sensation wasn't unpleasant at all. "Inside," she managed, her voice sounding raspy.

"Good choice," he said, then steered her into the house just enough so that the door closed. Then he cupped her chin, tilted her head up, and kissed her so gently she almost feared that she'd cry.

"Cam, I—"

"We have company," he said, nodding to the little

girl who now stood in the middle of the living area, her thumb in her mouth and her eyes wide. "Hey, kiddo," he added, then squatted down and held out his arms.

She raced into them, and he stood up quickly, holding her like a rag doll as she kicked and squealed. It was obviously a game they'd played before, and Mina moved to sit on the edge of the couch as she watched their easy playfulness.

"So what are you doing today?" He aimed the question at Faith, but he was looking at Mina.

"Puppies!" Faith said.

"We were going to the park," Mina explained. "After that, we were thinking lunch."

"Sounds like a good plan." He stood, then held out a hand for each of them. "Shall we?"

Brent had insisted she drive his car if she took Faith out, so she'd traded with him rather than have him use a ride share service to get downtown. Now, they buckled Faith into the pink car seat in the back of Brent's Volvo, then drove the short distance to the park.

There weren't many dogs, but an elderly man with a bouncy mutt that Faith obviously knew from other visits gave her a soggy tennis ball to throw. She spent a blissful half hour playing catch with Barclay the dog before moving on to join some other kids in the sandpit.

Mina and Cam watched her from a nearby bench, and after a while, he reached over and twined his fingers with hers. The last of the tension faded from her. She wasn't sure she completely understood what happened between them over the last twenty-four hours, but she was certain that this felt good.

For a moment, she simply sat there and soaked up his company, then he turned and asked, very simply, "What happened with Zach?"

She blinked, for the first time realizing that she didn't know, and she told him as much.

"He didn't come to the party? Did you ask Darryl why not?"

"No. I didn't think about it." Honestly, she'd been too busy cursing Tiffany to worry about some guy she hadn't wanted to meet in the first place.

Her mouth curved into a frown as she considered that, and she turned to face him more directly. "What was I right about? Yesterday, I mean, when you whispered in my ear?"

His mouth slid into a slow grin. "Wanting me."

She didn't deny it. "Confident much?"

"About some things."

She tilted her head, studying him. "What aren't you confident about?"

"I'm not confident you want me for the right reasons, for one."

"Oh." She pulled her hand back, then twisted her fingers together. "What do you mean?"

He didn't answer. Instead, he said, "If you don't want Darryl to know, I can live with that. But I'm not interested in being fuck buddies or friends with benefits or whatever cutesy new slang is floating around out there."

Her eyes widened and she couldn't keep the horror out of her voice. "Wait. No sex? Are you kidding me?"

He laughed, rich and deep. "I'm flattered the idea mortifies you so much. Frankly, it does me, too. No, I'm totally keeping sex on the table. But I want more." He studied her face as he spoke, and she wondered what he saw in her eyes.

Confusion, probably. Because this wasn't the Cam she thought she knew. And desire, because this was most definitely the Cam she wanted. A Cam who laid it out and took charge. Who had a plan, and went after it. Even if *she* was the plan.

Or maybe *especially* if she was the plan.

"What kind of more?" she asked after a beat.

"If we were in high school, I'd say that I want to go steady. Now, I think we can just call it dating."

"But you said we didn't have to tell Darryl—"

"We can be discreet. We're already friends. No one is going to blink if we're together. But I want to get past Christmas. And if all we have between us is sex, that's never going to happen."

"I'm not looking for a relationship," she said, his mention of her Christmas timeframe making her feel a little trapped.

"Fair enough. I'm not asking you to marry me." He took her hand and twined their fingers. "I want to hang out with *you*, Mina. Not your vagina. At least, not entirely," he added with a wry grin.

And in some weird way that was probably the nicest thing a man had ever said to her.

"Exclusive?"

"Hell to the yes," he said.

She cocked her head. "Tiffany?" she demanded, and realized from his expression that she'd been played. "You bastard. That wasn't a real date? It was all bullshit?"

"Hardly. It worked."

"Worked?"

"You were jealous."

"The hell I was," she lied. But since he so obviously knew she was lying, it didn't count.

"We've become pretty good friends over the last year. She helped me out. But don't worry, she won't tell Darryl. She's got her own secret to keep."

"Really?" Mina pondered that for a moment, playing back every memory of Tiff she could conjure from the bar, but didn't have a clue.

"Nope," he said when she prodded. "I promised."

And even though she *really* wanted to know, she couldn't fault his integrity.

When Faith trotted over and finished the last water bottle before complaining that her tummy was gurgling, they decided it was time to head back to the house. Rather than grab fast food, Cam made them peanut butter and jelly sandwiches with the crusts cut off, apple slices, and pudding cups.

Technically, he didn't make the pudding cups, but Mina was still impressed with his mad skills with regard to the care and feeding of children.

"Puppies?" Faith asked after finishing off the last of her milk. "Please?"

"Oh, sweetie, we just got back from the park." Now that she was back in the house, Mina realized she was zonked. Considering all she'd done was sit on a bench in a park and then sit on a stool in the kitchen, she had nothing to complain about. But, honestly, childcare was hard, and her respect for Brent shot up a few more notches.

"Damnations," Faith protested, as Mina's eyes widened with surprise that bubbled into laughter.

"Dalmatians," she corrected. "And if you know where your dad keeps the DVD, we can put it on."

It turned out not to be a DVD, it was a digital movie, and Faith had the TV on and found the video in five seconds flat. Soon, she was happily ensconced on the couch, with Mina and Cam on either side of her. She wiggled and squirmed as she got sleepier, and eventually she was lying across them, her head in Mina's lap, and her legs sprawled across Cameron.

Since the one thing that Mina was certain of about childcare was that kids without naps could be grumpy little beasts, she feared moving Faith and waking her. So they stayed on the couch, their hands clasped on the little girl's back, as they finished watching the movie.

It was the last reprieve before Faith's bedtime. She woke from her nap completely invigorated. And between stories, baking cookies, playing chase in the backyard, and building a massive pillow fort, she ran both Mina and Cam ragged. So much so that when

Brent got home at just before three in the morning, he found his daughter and her babysitters asleep on top of a pile of pillows that had only recently been a massive Scottish keep.

"Just stay," Brent said when Mina peeled her eyes open. "I'll fix breakfast in the morning."

And Mina, who was still half-asleep and too exhausted to argue, nodded, pressed one hand on Faith's back, took Cam's hand with her other, and fell back to sleep.

Chapter Nine

"I'VE BARELY SEEN you or my sister since Saturday," Darryl said on Wednesday when he slid into the booth opposite Cameron at Pizza Mambo, a new pizza by the slice place just a few blocks from the Federal Building.

"She wrangled me into babysitting with her. Although, technically, I think Brent wrangled her into babysitting a few more days than she'd originally planned."

"Brent. That's the security guy, right? The cute one?"

"Yes, and if you say so. And before you ask, I'm pretty sure he's straight. And I definitely know he has no time for anything but work and his kid."

Darryl took a sip of his Dr. Pepper. "Considering how busy the judge has me already, I'm pretty sure I won't be dating until after my clerkship."

"But you like it?"

"Yeah, it's great. The judge and the other clerks are

terrific." He lifted a shoulder. "But even if they weren't, it would be worth it. A Federal Clerkship is resume gold."

Cam nodded, but he was thinking of Mina and her laser-like focus on getting to LA. As far as she was concerned, the Austin job she'd be starting soon was only a stepping-stone to bigger and better things, even though the small studio had a successful record and an impressive team.

Of course, Cam knew the twins' father, so he knew how important career was in the family. And he'd also seen the way father and brother doted on Mina. And, frankly, he understood the need to succeed. To live up to the bar set by a parent or, in his case, an older sibling.

Still, he couldn't help but think her career path was a road that led far, far away from him. He just didn't know how long it would be before she started walking it.

Christmas, a little voice in his head whispered. And even though he knew that they'd moved past that conversation—and even though she'd pulled the date out of a hat in the first place—he couldn't help but feel like the end was already barreling down on them even though they'd only barely gotten started.

"—you into it."

"Sorry," Cam said. "What?"

"I said thanks for letting her drag you into it. Even though I'm confident she could handle a five-year-old, I'm sure it's a lot easier with you along."

"It's been fun, too. Over the last couple of days, we took Faith ice-skating, to the Children's Museum, to the zoo, and we rented a paddleboat. Basically, we wore the poor kid out. But she loved it."

He'd loved it, too. Mostly because every day when they'd returned to Brent's house, Faith conked out. Which meant that he and Mina had plenty of time to talk on the couch or drink coffee on the back porch or just watch a movie while they recovered from dealing with a five-year-old.

They'd held hands and laughed together, and it had felt ridiculously domestic and wonderful. And while he had no desire for kids of his own yet, there was a sweetness to the situation that had bubbled inside him, like a shiny promise for the future that he could tuck away.

A promise that became more and more tarnished whenever he thought about Mina's stated goal to get to LA, and her plan to use her upcoming job in Austin as a stepping stone.

But that was a long way off. She didn't even start the job for another week, and the point was to get experience. She wouldn't even begin looking for LA-based jobs for at least a year, maybe two.

And who knew what could happen in a year? Hell, so much had already happened in only a week.

Like, for example, the fact that he was absolutely, totally, one hundred percent falling in love with Mina Silver.

Not that he was surprised by that revelation. After all, he'd been half in love with her his entire life. But what he felt now was no teenage crush. It was rich and deep. Desire mixed with admiration and respect and longing and a connection so intense that when she was away from him he missed her with a physical ache. And not merely the sexual kind, though he wouldn't deny he had that kind of craving as well.

They hadn't made love since the weekend of Darryl's party, and Cam was fine with that. Their sweet courtship had solidified his feelings, and, he hoped, made Mina see *him*, and not just a good time.

The hard part was that he wanted to tell Mina how he felt, but he feared scaring her off. And now, after years of hiding his crush from Darryl, Cam desperately wanted his friend's advice, since no one knew Mina better than her twin. But he'd promised Mina, and so he held his tongue.

"Have you seen her today?" Cam asked. "Do you know if she got that paper done?" She'd spent a good chunk of Tuesday on her laptop in Brent's house finalizing the cinematography article she'd been writing for publication with one of her advisors.

"She came into the house for breakfast," Darryl told him. "Said she hadn't had time to hit the grocery store and needed eggs. And yeah. She said she finished and was meeting with the professor right after lunch to go over it one last time."

"And you? What's on your agenda today? Anything after work?"

Darryl frowned. "I was hoping to go for a bike ride, but I'm going to end up working late. Want to go down to the Veloway this weekend?"

Cam nodded. "Sure." Frankly, he could use the exercise. He'd blown off all his recent training sessions at the gym with Matthew. Fortunately, he'd gotten quite a workout chasing Faith.

"I'm back on the clock at the Fix starting Friday," he told Darryl, "but my shift doesn't start until six."

Darryl was an avid biker, and though Cam knew he preferred the city streets, considering the mess that was Austin traffic, Cam would much rather bike on the path.

"Are you biking to work?" It was a trek from Darryl's house to the downtown Federal Building, but Cam knew that was nothing for Darryl.

"Maybe when the weather gets cooler. Right now, I'm too focused on making a good impression on my judge. I don't need to be juggling clothes, too. Speaking of, I need to get back." He pointed a finger at Cam. "Saturday," he said. "I'll pick you up. I've got a rack on the back of the Land Rover."

They finalized the plans and paid the bill, then walked out together. And although Cam had every intention of heading back to his room in the West Campus co-op, he somehow ended up in the open area in front of the main doors to the film school.

Which was ridiculous, since even during summer the University of Texas was an ant bed of activity, and the odds of him bumping into Mina were incredibly slim. For all he knew, she and the professor had finished hours ago, and she was at The Domain shopping with one of her girlfriends. Or she and the professor had gone to the Student Union to have a drink while they went over the article line by line.

He tugged his phone out of his back pocket, intending to tell her he was on campus, and to ping him back if she was free. Then he'd walk back to the co-op slowly, just in case he heard from her.

He didn't get the chance.

"Cam!"

He turned toward the sound of her voice, and when he saw her delighted smile, he felt as if he'd been lit by a beam of sunlight.

"What are you doing here?" she asked as she hurried to his side.

"Would it sound stalker-ish if I said I wanted to see you?"

Her smile widened and a tint of pink bloomed on her cheeks. "Absolutely. But in a kinder, gentler stalker way."

He laughed, then took her hand. "Are you free for the rest of the day?"

She frowned, looking genuinely disappointed. "I told Megan and Taylor we could do shopping then drinks at The Domain. What?" she added, obviously seeing his grin.

"Not a thing," he said, though he'd predicted that very scenario. "Tell them I said hello. What about tomorrow night?"

"That I can do so long as it's after seven."

"Hot date?"

She tilted her head up to meet his eyes, the heat in hers just about melting him. "Well, I certainly hope so."

"I think I can pretty much guarantee that after seven. Before, you're on your own."

"Not too much in the way of excitement there. I'm taking the handheld around The Fix before it gets too crowded. Just to make sure the editors have enough background footage. But why don't you meet me there? Have you got something in mind for the evening?"

He paused, then made it a point to rake his eyes over her, very slowly and very thoroughly. "Yeah," he said. "I do."

"Oh. Well, good." She took his hand. "I'm free for a couple of hours. Isn't your co-op around here?"

"Actually, I have another idea."

"Yeah? What?"

"Trust me," he said, pleased when she acquiesced without begging him for details of what he had in mind. Not even when their first stop was the Student Union, where he bought a bag of raw sunflower seeds. Then he led the way through the maze of roads and buildings as they headed east toward the law school, stopping period-ically to feed the always-eager squirrels.

Apparently the critters had some sort of wireless communication system, because word travelled, and every time they sat to feed one, more and more came. So that by the time they reached the grounds by the law school they were out of nuts and, Mina decided, getting the stink-eye from the still-hungry legal squirrels.

"They're ridiculously cute," she said. "And God forbid one decides to move off-campus. I can't imagine a more pampered squirrel population anywhere in the world."

"When I was little, Grandma used to bring Kiki and me here. We didn't have much money, so the University was like a playground. We'd have massive picnics on the hill by the LBJ Library and commune with the squirrels and the birds. It's one of the reasons I wanted to go to school here," he added with a shrug. "It's always felt like home."

"Why are we at the law school?" she asked. "You decide to follow my brother's career path after all?"

"A million times no. But I do want to level the playing field."

Her brows rose in question.

"I see a bit of what you do. The camera. Helping with the lighting. I kind of get it."

"Again I ask, why the law school?"

"The Tarlton Law Library has a rare books and manuscripts archive. I want to show you something. After the squirrels, I figure you'll think it's interesting. At the very least, you'll think it's cute."

"Well, now I really am intrigued. Lead the way."

He did, taking her into the huge, quiet library with its open stacks of law books and glass cases of artifacts. The librarians knew him, as he'd spent a good portion of the last year in the rare book collection working on various papers and projects.

He led the way back to the rare books room, where he met Kelly, one of the archivists. He'd texted ahead while they'd been feeding the squirrels, and she'd already put out the book that he wanted Mina to see. She greeted them, reminded Cam to use the cotton gloves if he touched anything, then melted into her office, reflecting a trust that humbled him. The books in this room really were priceless.

"It's beautiful," Mina said, her voice low and reverent. She stood at the end of the table, her hands behind her back as if to remind herself not to touch the thick bound book open to two pages filled with intricate drawings and almost indecipherable calligraphy. "Is it a Gutenberg Bible?"

"No, the Gutenberg Bibles were printed on a printing press. This is an illuminated manuscript, and this one was handwritten in the thirteen hundreds."

She tilted her head up to look at him. "Really? All of it?"

He nodded. "Monks would copy the pages, day after day after day."

"Tedious."

"Yup. Check this out." This was the part that always amused the middle school kids that sometimes toured the library. "When they got bored, they'd doodle."

He indicated the margin, and she bent closer. "Is that a mouse?" She looked up at him. "The monk drew a mouse?"

He grinned, more at her delight than at the mouse. "Cool isn't it? And some manuscripts have some pretty racy images in the margins, too."

He showed her a bit more from the collection, thrilled that she seemed genuinely interested. When they finally left the library and could speak in a normal tone and not worry about where they put their hands, she slid into his arms and sighed.

"Thanks," she said. "I like seeing a bit of what you do."

"It's not all monks and mice," he said, making her laugh.

"No, I get that. But it's a peek inside of you. And I like that." She rose up on her toes and kissed him then, casually and sweetly. A gentle kiss. Tender and soft and loving.

It was the kind of kiss that felt like a relationship.

But even as his heart twisted with joy, Cam knew better than to get his hopes up.

Chapter Ten

CAM WOKE before five a.m. to the sound of his phone ringing, the shrill sound rocketing him to consciousness. He snatched the phone, afraid it was Mina, then sagged in relief when he saw Kiki's number.

"Time goes the *other* way," he said.

"Shit! I'm sorry. I wasn't thinking. Are you awake?"

"Well, I am now," he grumbled. "Are you still in London?" His sister was the lead singer and songwriter with Pink Chameleon, a band that had recently made a comeback, and was now touring the United States and Europe to great reviews and sell-out crowds.

"Yup. Celia and I are walking through the park outside Buckingham Palace."

"Tell Noah he needs to do a better job monitoring your phone use," he said, the comment making her laugh. Her husband of almost two years now, Noah was the President of the Austin division of Stark Applied

Technology. With Kiki on tour, though, he was doing a lot of work from the road.

"He's in New York with Damien," she said, referring to the head of the company, Damien Stark, a man Cam had only met a couple of times, but found to be ridiculously down to earth considering he could probably buy the entire solar system and then some. "I'm not going to see him until we meet up in Austin."

"Well, then tell him to make you a cheat sheet, because every time he's away, you call me in the middle of the—*wait*. Did you say Austin?"

"Yup. We've squeezed in performances in Dallas and San Antonio at the beginning of the second leg of the US tour. And I insisted that we have at least one night at home. This on the road thing is crazy pants."

"That's fabulous." Technically his half-sister by a different father, Kiki was ten years older than him. She'd been as much a mom as a sister, and he'd been thrilled when she moved to Austin—and missed her terribly now that she was on the road. "When will you be here?"

"Dallas is Tuesday. San Antonio is Thursday. I intend to sleep in my very own bed on Wednesday night."

"Wednesday?" he repeated. "That's not even a week away."

"I know. Plan on dinner."

"Hell, yeah, I will. I—oh. Shit."

"You have plans." He heard the disappointment in her voice.

"Kind of. You remember I told you about the calendar guy contest at The Fix?"

"Comic relief," she said, and he could practically hear her rolling her eyes. "I can't believe you did that."

"I can't believe I told you," he said dryly. "At any rate, the contest is every other week, which puts Mr. March on this coming Wednesday."

"And you're entering again?"

"Hell, no," he said quickly. "Well, technically, I'm already entered since all the guys can roll over to the next contest if they don't win. But no. That's not my plan. But Mina's working the show, and since I'm an assistant manager now, I figure I should be there even if it's not my shift."

"That's right. I already said congratulations when you texted me, but congrats again."

"Thanks again."

"And what about Mina?"

He'd confessed the crush to Kiki before she'd gone on tour, figuring that she might have some brilliant, life-changing advice.

She hadn't, but just sharing his feelings with his sister had been a relief.

"Things are good," he told her now, then gave her the PG-rated rundown of his recent time with Mina. "Actually, I was going to text you when I got up and ask you—"

He'd intended to ask about using their downtown condo for a date with Mina, but cut himself off as a brilliant idea swelled in his head.

"Cam?"

"Is it just you and Noah coming to Austin? Or is the whole band coming?"

"Just me and Noah. Celia has family in San Antonio, and Eden and Kristi said they want to fall face down on a hotel mattress and sleep until we perform. Why?"

"Would you be willing to do an acoustic number? Just you and your guitar? I know you can't do the songs you're touring with, but maybe something you're working on?".

"Um, I guess. Why?"

"Well, it would be a great surprise for all the customers. I mean, it's been well over a year since you've performed here, and that was before the band got huge. And I could get Nolan to talk about it afterwards on his radio show. And then word would get out that The Fix is the kind of place where Kiki King drops in to perform, and that would get it on the map. And since we're trying to increase revenue, I figure—"

"I get it," she said, laughter in her voice. "And sure. I can do that. On one condition."

He narrowed his eyes, even though she couldn't see him. "What?"

"You enter the calendar contest."

It was a good thing he was still in bed, because that demand would have laid him flat. "Seriously? Why?"

"Honestly, because I've been on the road for what seems like forever, I've missed you, and I haven't given you enough shit lately."

He rubbed his temples, then sighed. Because how

the hell could he argue with that? "Fine. I'm in. But *I* have a condition."

"Good God, this could go on forever. What's yours?"

"I'm taking Mina out tonight. Can I take her back to your condo?"

"Of course. You have all the access codes."

"I know. I just wanted to ask. And is it okay to stay through the weekend?"

"Planning one hell of a date, are we?"

"Not planning so much as hoping," he admitted, making her laugh.

"Again, you don't even have to ask. So long as you're out before we get there on Wednesday, consider it yours."

DESPITE GOING BACK to sleep after he hung up with Kiki, Cam was exhausted by the time six o'clock rolled around. Mostly because he'd spent the afternoon running various errands and making trip after trip to the condo in order to get everything just the way he wanted.

Only when he was certain that everything was perfect, and he'd forgotten nothing, did he finally shower and change into clean jeans and a button-down shirt, then walk the few blocks from Kiki and Noah's downtown condo to The Fix on Sixth.

It was only six-fifteen when he arrived, but that was okay. If Mina wasn't finished, Cam was happy to hang out and talk with his friends.

He headed straight for the bar where Eric was busy working, then he glanced around until he caught Tiffany's eye. She gave him a thumbs-up, but whether that was her way of saying hello or a signal that things were going well with Eric, Cam didn't know.

Not that it mattered. Tiffany was too busy to ask, and Cam was preoccupied with finding both Mina and Jenna. He found Mina first; she was walking the perimeter, her camera scanning the room. He could tell the second she noticed him, because she stopped moving, kept the camera on him, and grinned. He assumed she'd zoomed in on him, and he made a goofy face, causing her to lower the camera and stick her tongue out at him.

He winked, then continued his search for Jenna, ultimately finding her in the office with Tyree going over a stack of paperwork.

"Cam, my man," Ty said, shifting his attention from the paper to the doorway as Cam knocked on the frame. "A little eager, aren't you? You're not on shift until tomorrow."

"I can't stay away from this place," Cam said, and Tyree's smile broadened.

"I know that feeling. What's up?"

"I was looking for Jenna, but you'll both want to hear this." He told them about his conversation with Kiki and about her agreement to perform before the Mr. March contest.

"Are you shitting me?" Tyree said. "Because if you are, that's grounds for firing."

"Funny," Cam said, as Tyree leaned back in his chair, his hands behind his head.

"Damn, but I always did like your sister."

"No kidding," Jenna said. "I'm talking major girl-crush here. She's really okay with that? Because this is amazing."

"Totally okay. She loves this bar, and she likes small venues with just her guitar way more than the monster stadiums her managers set up for the band's tours."

"What's going on?" Mina asked, coming up behind him and putting her hand on the flat of his back.

For a second, Cam stiffened, certain she'd realize the intimacy of the touch and step back, but she kept her hand there, although she did ease forward so that she was standing beside him.

"Kiki's going to perform next Wednesday," Jenna said.

"No kidding?" She looked at Cam. "You arranged that?"

"I might have had something to do with it."

For the flicker of an instant, their eyes met, and he saw the tiniest smile play at her lips. Then she turned to Jenna. "I came to tell you that Brooke had a question. And to let you know I'm heading out. I've got a hot date tonight."

She didn't look at him. Just turned and left, her hand falling away from his back and leaving a Mina-shaped handprint of heat and promise.

Jenna looked after her, then turned her attention to him. For a second, he thought she was going to say something about him and Mina. But then her gaze dropped to the desktop, she grabbed a leather folio, and hurried past him into the hall saying, "I'll go see what Brooke needs."

Cam told Tyree that he was heading out, too, and if Tyree made the connection between him and Mina, he didn't show it. All he said was, "You earned yourself some serious karma, Cam my man. Thanks."

Cam nodded in acknowledgement, then walked back toward the main bar, intent on finding Mina.

He didn't get that far. Instead, Mina grabbed him by the elbow and pulled him into the dark corner near the shelves where the paper products were stored. "That was nice what you did," she said. "Asking your sister to perform, I mean."

"You think?"

She hooked her hands around his neck and lifted herself up on her toes. Her lips brushed his ear as she whispered. "Very take charge. Very sexy."

He stifled a moan, the unexpected sensation of her breath tickling his ear wreaking wonderful havoc with his insides. "Mina," he murmured, surprised and aroused. Anyone could come back here. Anyone could see. And the moment they did, the secret was over.

Which was fine by him, but the fact that Mina was being so reckless was such a turn-on that he was as hard as steel...and seriously considering abandoning all of his careful plans in order to yank her out into the alley and fuck her senseless right then.

Her hand slid down to cup his cock, and she made a

soft noise of satisfaction that only made him harder. "I have high hopes for our date," she teased.

"I'll try hard to live up to your expectations," he retorted, stressing the word hard and making her laugh as her hand pressed against him even more firmly.

He groaned, then roughly took her wrists and pushed her back against the wall, her hands forced above her head as he pressed his body against hers. "You're playing a dangerous game, baby. Because I swear I'm on the verge of taking you right here, propriety and job security and our secret be damned."

"The ladies room is just across the hall. It has a lock."

Christ.

She squirmed but he held her hands firm, sorely tempted.

So ridiculously, incredibly, painfully tempted.

"No," he finally said, then almost changed his mind when he saw the disappointment in her eyes. He leaned forward, releasing one wrist so that he could slide his hand down. He caressed her breast, then cupped her sex over the spandex of her leggings as she ground down on his hand. "Anticipation," he murmured, then eased back, breaking the contact between them.

"Bastard," she said.

"For now," he agreed. "But I bet you won't think so soon." He trailed his fingertip down her neck, over her collarbone, then lower and lower, veering off before he reached her sex. "I think you'll be begging me for more."

She nodded, her green eyes flashing with both sensual heat and challenge. "All right then," she said. "Prove it. Let's see if you can make me melt."

Chapter Eleven

"A LIMO?" Mina stopped on the street to look at the sleek, black vehicle. They'd left The Fix through the back door and then walked down the alley to Brazos Street. She hadn't thought anything of the limo at first, but then the driver had stepped out and held the door open, and Cam had steered her that direction.

Now, as she slipped into the dark interior, she looked over her shoulder at Cam and smiled, a little bit awed. "Unexpected, but nice."

He settled in beside her as the driver indicated the two freshly poured Mimosas. Cam handed Mina hers before pushing the button on the privacy screen and picking up his own glass. "To surprises," he said, and a laugh bubbled out of her. The truth was, Cam was the biggest surprise of all. The way she felt so easy with him. So connected.

"Definitely." She clinked his glass then took a sip before looking out the window. "Where are we going?"

"Are you fuzzy on the definition of surprise?"

She finished her mimosa and held her glass out with her brows raised, challenging him to deny her another. "Silly me. I thought the limo was the surprise."

"It's a multipart surprise," he told her as he made her a fresh drink. "Part of the surprise is traveling in style."

"You got that right. This is a sweet ride. My dad hardly ever hires limos, and when he does, it's for work. The only ones I've ever been in were during school. And those reeked of beer. And usually had a half-naked frat guy with his head through the sunroof screaming drunken insults at pedestrians."

This, she thought was much better. A nice ride and an even nicer guy. And the two of them all alone with all sorts of possibilities.

"Damn," he said. "I forgot to arrange for the drunken frat guy." He pointed to the sunroof. "Shall I start to strip down?"

"Later," she said. "I think you can count on it." She looked him slowly up and down, and then licked her lips for effect. "But I think I'll keep you in the limo and all to myself."

She asked where they were going, but he told her that was part of the surprise.

"I grew up here, too, you know," she said. "Surprise destinations aren't going to be that easy unless you're taking me to the airport."

"Damn. I forgot to reserve the jet to Paris."

She had a sudden vision of the two of them in Paris,

eating croissants from a street cafe, holding hands as the rode up the Eiffel Tower, exploring the Louvre and all the winding streets in the city.

With his sense of fun and his love of history, it would be an amazing trip, and it scared her a little how much she wanted to start seriously planning just such a journey.

He pulled her close then and kissed her, distracting her from her Parisian fantasies and ensuring that she lost all interest in trying to figure out where they were going. Instead, they wiled away the time enjoying a time-honored limo tradition—making out in privacy in the very back seat.

Once the car stopped, she was distracted by the need to straighten her clothes, and so she didn't realize where they were until the driver opened the door and she recognized the well-known Austin restaurant.

"The Oasis!" she said, thrilled with his choice. "And just in time for sunset. This couldn't be more perfect."

"I'm friends with one of the bartenders, and he promised he'd make sure the hostess seats us at a perfect table."

She knew what he meant by perfect, of course. The Oasis was built in multiple levels on a hill over-looking Lake Travis. It faced the west, and the sunsets over the water were both stunning and well-known. Getting a primo table, especially in the summer, was quite a feat.

"You're amazing. A limo and perfect seats. What will you think of next?"

"Actually, margaritas and nachos if that sounds good to you."

"Are you kidding? It's perfect." She squeezed his hand across the table. "This is perfect."

They still had thirty minutes until sunset, and they talked about everything and nothing—including her fantasy Paris trip—as the sun slipped lower and lower in the sky, finally disappearing in a cacophony of color.

"That was amazing," she said. "This date has been amazing."

"I'm glad you approve," he said, flashing a crooked grin. "But it's not over yet."

In fact, she thought an hour later, the Oasis had barely been an appetizer. After they returned to downtown, he took her to one of the high-rise condo buildings, and they rode up, up, up until finally entering a small studio with a view of the river. "It'll be gorgeous tomorrow," he said, "but even at night it's pretty with the lights."

She nodded agreement as she explored the place, noticing the soft classical music and the wine glasses already out on the bar by the kitchen area.

The bedroom was an area set off by bookcases, and she saw the bedspread was pulled back and rose petals decorated the sheets.

"I'll bite," she said. "What's going on. Is this your place?"

"Ours," he said. "Just for the weekend."

"Don't you work this weekend? And how is it ours?"

"It's my sister's. Well, hers and Noah's. This was his

place before they got married, and he kept it. They have a house in LA, too. And so long as we clear out before they get here on Wednesday, we have the run of the place."

"But—"

"And you're right. I have to work. But I thought it would be nice to share a place—to just share everyday life—for a couple of days. But if you think it's a stupid idea or if it makes you uncomfortable—"

"I like it," she interrupted, rushing to reassure him. And she really did. "Yes," she said, holding out her hands to him. "I want to play house with you, Cameron Reed."

The relief on his face was so obvious that she was overcome with the urge to kiss him. And since there was no reason not to, that's exactly what she did. Then she put her arms around him and held him close, feeling happy and spoiled and loved.

"I have a bottle of wine chilling," he said. "Do you want some?"

She nodded, then took a seat in front of the window while he brought over the glasses and the white wine. They watched the lights of the neighborhoods beyond the river, and talked about their plans for the weekend. He told her how to get into the condo and asked what she'd do while he was at work.

She almost said she was going to pick up stray men and bring them to the condo, but even though it was so obviously a joke, she couldn't conjure the words. She didn't want even a joking thought about another man coming between them.

He was, she realized, all she wanted. And the thought was less scary than it should have been. After all, she'd never expected to feel so serious about a guy. Not yet anyway. Not until she was older and more established in her career.

But what they had felt right. Good. She just wasn't sure if she could trust the way it felt. Or even if she should let him into her heart since she'd be off to Los Angeles as soon as she had enough experience under her belt.

Then again, it was too late for that. He *was* in her heart. Her heart and her head and her thoughts. And no matter what came next, she didn't want that to change. She didn't know if she was in love with him, and she wasn't quite ready to think about that. But she did know that she wanted him. That being with him felt right.

And that, she supposed, was plenty to be going on with.

"Hey, you got quiet," he said. "Penny for your thoughts?"

"They're worth at least a quarter," she countered.

"Deal."

"I was thinking about you," she admitted, then stood up and held out her hand to him. "And I was thinking about the bed and the rose petals. And," she added, as she tugged him that direction, "I was thinking that I really want you to make love to me now."

And of course, since Cam was a gentleman, he did exactly what she asked.

BY LATE SUNDAY–TECHNICALLY Monday—Cam knew that he owed his sister big time. He'd never felt more at ease than he had sharing the studio with Mina. They walked on the trail by the river in the mornings, then came back to the condo for breakfast and made love in the shower. She spent a few hours each day at The Fix helping Brooke and Spencer, but they still had plenty of time for a quick dinner before he went in for his shift.

And since they were both used to crazy bar hours, they made love again in the wee hours after he came home from work. Then they lazed together in bed and caught each other up on their days, him telling her all about his new managerial position—which was harder work than bartending, but worth it—and her telling him about articles she'd read, places she'd visited, and all the little things she was doing as she enjoyed her free time between school and her new job that was starting soon.

That intimacy was what he was most looking forward to now as he rode the elevator up after his shift. And he called out her name as he stepped inside.

Usually, she greeted him with a sparkling water, but today she only waved from where she sat at the kitchen table with her phone to her ear and a cup of coffee in front of her.

"Thanks," she was saying. "I really am excited. It couldn't be a better opportunity." She nodded. "Yeah, really soon. I don't know—oh, that's terrific. I can't believe you forgot to tell me that right off the bat. An actual producing credit?"

She stood as she listened, then came over to kiss him, signaling that she'd only be another minute. "Well, tell him I said congratulations and that we'll talk soon. I know, right? Definitely happy hour worthy. Okay, love you, too. Bye!"

She ended the call, then moved into the kitchen to fill her mug.

"One of your LA friends?" he asked.

"Lydia," she said, her back to him. "She moved to LA after undergrad and is doing really well. And she told me that another friend of ours just got his first producing credit."

"And you told them about your job, I hope."

"Yeah," she said, her voice a little hollow. "That's actually why I called her. I know it's late there, but with the time difference, I knew she'd still be up."

He frowned, not certain why, but feeling like there was something off in her voice. "She must know the studio," he said. "I mean, with projects from both Griffin and Beverly Martin on their dance card, you're going to work for a real competitor."

"I know." She finally turn around, then rubbed her face, looking tired. "It's just been a long, weird day, and I miss her. There was a group of us that did drinks every Friday night. Call it late night melancholy. Actually," she said, "don't call it anything at all. Because I'm going to shake off this mood."

A ball of worry had settled in his gut, but he was determined to shake that off, too. So he didn't ask her for more details. All he said was, "you're in luck. I know just how to do that. Get dressed," he added, his eyes skimming over the tiny tank top and sleep shorts that he loved seeing her in. "I want to show you something."

"What? Outside?"

Since she was already tugging her jeans back on, he didn't bother answering. He just waited for her to finish, then led the way to the door.

"It's almost three in the morning," she pointed out as they descended in the elevator. "Where are we going?"

"Not far," he promised. He'd called the car service again, and the limo was right on time, the driver standing by the door ready to hold it open for Mina.

"Good evening," he said as they both slipped inside, and Cam was pleased to see the driver hadn't forgotten a thing.

As the driver shut the door, Cam took one of the freshly poured Mimosas and handed it to Mina. "To long nights and wonderful company," he said.

She still looked baffled, but she smiled broadly, then clinked her glass against his. "I'll drink to that." She took a sip, then nodded at the two small canvas bags on the floor. They were both zipped shut with no logo. "Are those for us?"

"Yup."

"Can I open one?"

"Nope."

"Cam!"

He laughed, amused by her confusion. Soon enough she'd have her answer, and in fact, they'd barely been in the car for five minutes when the driver pulled over at the designated spot on Baylor Street at the edge of downtown, just below the old castle. "Come on," Cam said, grabbing his bag and urging Mina to pick up hers.

"Graffiti Park!" She looked around, delighted. "Do you know I've never been here?"

"Me neither," Cam admitted, but he knew about it. Most Austinites did. Officially called the Hope Outdoor Gallery, Graffiti Park consisted of the concrete remnants of old buildings at the bottom of a hill. An urban contrast to the medieval-style castle that graced the hilltop, one of the earliest buildings in Austin, and which Cam had been in once as a kid when the then-owners had turned it into a haunted house for Halloween.

For years, the slabs had stood stark white, like bones rotting in the sun. Then after a South-by-Southwest event in 2011, it was opened to muralists. After that, it evolved as a venue for taggers, with the graffiti being periodically whitewashed so that folks could start over.

Now, it was completely covered by layer upon layer of art on top of art. And Cam intended to add one more layer.

"They're about to demolish it," he said. "I'm not sure exactly when, but I read that the city council voted on it, and it's going to be torn down, and maybe part of it relocated out by the airport." He shrugged. "I guess the folks in the neighborhood don't like the crowds it draws."

"Too bad," she said. "It's pretty cool."

They started climbing until they found a slab with mostly solid colors. Mina opened her bag, found a can of white paint, and sprayed, *Mina & Cam Were Here*, then proceeded to spray smiley faces and little stick figures.

They both sprayed goofy images for a while, demonstrating their complete lack of artistic skill, until finally Cam took her hand and pulled her to one side. "This," he said, then very carefully sprayed *Mina + Cam 4ever* inside a large, red heart.

When he was done, he turned to look at her, his heart pounding because he knew he'd laid it on the line.

But her hand was pressed to her chest and her expression was wistful, and when she turned and smiled at him, his shoulders sagged with relief. At least until she stepped over to him, took his hand, and sighed.

"Forever," she whispered. "At least until they knock the place down."

Chapter Twelve

CAM SAT on the edge of the bed, every nerve in his body crackling with heat and anticipation as he glanced toward the bathroom door. She was back there. *Mina.* And as he waited for her to come out, he couldn't help but think that he had no idea how he'd gotten so lucky to have finally won her.

But he had. She was his. *His.*

He swallowed, nerves tingling as he waited. He was hyperaware of everything. The buzz of the air conditioner. The silk of the bedspread. The sound of the water running in the bathroom.

And then—*oh, God*—the subtle click of the doorknob turning and the creak of hinges as the bathroom door opened.

She stepped out, clad in a short terrycloth robe that ended at the top of her thighs and revealed miles of perfect legs. She walked toward him, and he swallowed, knowing without seeing that she was naked underneath.

That all she had to do was loosen the tie at her waist and open the robe to reveal herself to him. Her firm breasts, her flat belly, her entire body that he'd come to know so well but could never get enough of.

"I'm ready," she whispered, and he felt his cock go hard.

He nodded, his mouth too dry to speak. And when she took another step toward him and pulled loose the sash, he thought his heart might stop.

But that was nothing compared to when her hands went to the robe, and she started to pull it open. To reveal herself to him. To stand naked before him and—

Bang!

A wave of golden light burst from the robe, blinding him and knocking him backward.

And when he'd blinked enough to clear his vision, she was gone—and so was the entire apartment.

He was left standing alone among white concrete slabs, sun bleached and cracked. All except one that stood in the middle, a single phrase sprayed on it in bold, curvy lettering:

Forever only lasts until it's over.

———

CAM SAT BOLT UPRIGHT, his heart pounding as the dream lingered.

Beside him, Mina blinked and rose up onto her elbow, then reached for him, her warm hand on his managing to calm him. "Hey. Are you okay?"

He nodded, forcing himself to breath normally. "Nightmare," he said, then rubbed his palms over his face. "Christ. That was—" He broke off with a shake of his head.

"Do you want to talk about it?"

"No," he said quickly. And then he took a deep breath and tried again. "No, it was just a stupid dream."

That was the truth, wasn't it? His dream was because of what she'd said at the park. Because he'd let himself believe that they'd gotten past her fears and hesitations, and those quixotic words had snuck into his subconscious, making him fear that he'd been deluding himself.

And hell, maybe he was.

After all, she still hadn't told Darryl that they were dating. And she still dreamed of working in Hollywood.

He'd been living a lust-filled dream with her, but except for amazing and regular sex, they were right where they were when they'd started. Nothing had changed at all.

Except it had.

The little voice in his head stressed the point again. *It had.*

And maybe that was true. They were together, after all. They had a connection.

For all intents and purposes, they were a couple.

Hell, maybe if he brought it up again, she'd be just fine telling Darryl. After all, it wasn't as if they'd talked about it recently.

"Hey," she murmured, her voice heavy with sleep. "You're really upset. You want to talk about it?"

He shook his head. "No. It just got under my skin."

"Well, come here." She lifted the sheet, inviting him back under, then spooned up next to him. "Better now?"

"Much better," he said. And he hoped like hell it was true.

"I'M NOT WORKING TONIGHT," Cam said on Monday morning as they scurried around the condo, gathering up their personal belongings and putting the place back in order for Kiki and Noah. They weren't arriving until Wednesday, but Cam wanted to clear out today so that the housekeeper could do a thorough cleaning. "Do you want to see if Darryl's up for a movie night? I could handle a wild action flick."

"Sure," she said, her voice muffled since she was on her hands and knees searching for a lost sock under the bed. "Come on, you," she muttered. "Show yourself."

Cam pressed his palm to his mouth to stifle a laugh, then leaned against the wall and watched her. He wanted to capture each and every memory. Because as much as the sex was great—and it was—these were the moments that he truly cherished. The little things that filled the days and made him smile.

The way she talked to herself when she gathered her clothes, which were inevitably scattered across the house. The way she hummed when she brushed her teeth, classical music on the weekends, and The Beatles during the week.

And he definitely loved the way she leaned casually against him as she waited for the bread to pop out of the toaster.

Real stuff. Real life.

That's what he wanted to wrap a bow around and keep forever, and that was what her comment at the park and the later dream had made him fear he was losing. The entirety of the woman he loved, not the girl he slept with. The nitty-gritty. Every tiny, unexplored piece that he could spend a lifetime discovering.

That's what he wanted—and he hoped she felt the same way. Because he couldn't stay hidden any longer. He wanted her. He wanted *them*. All weekend he'd had to censor his conversations at work, being careful not to reveal who'd he'd been with. And, dammit, he'd hated it.

He wanted to be a couple. For now and, God willing, forever.

He just hoped that when he told her as much he'd get his wish—and not one hell of a kick in the balls.

Chapter Thirteen

MINA HAD SEARCHED every square inch of the condo, and was certain she'd found every stray piece of clothing she'd misplaced over their long weekend in luxury. Which meant that she no longer had any reason for staying well-below Cam's eye level.

And since he was off the clock until Friday, he was no longer working crazy hours and dealing with managerial responsibilities. Any knotty problems she threw at him wouldn't be one more burden piled on an already challenging day.

In other words, Mina was all out of excuses.

She really wished she weren't. Because the talk they needed to have wasn't a talk she wanted to have. But Wednesday was coming up fast, and she was running out of time.

Dammit.

Her Los Angeles dream job had landed in her lap in the form of her new boss's outgoing personal assistant calling on Sunday afternoon to offer her the pie-in-the-sky job she'd applied for a full three months ago. *Hollywood*. The Holy Grail she'd dreamt about forever. The Shangri-La where her classmates were making films and building careers.

As far as Mina was concerned, she was at the center of a full-blown miracle, and the one person she wanted to share her news with was the one person who wouldn't want to hear it. Which was why she'd ended up calling Lydia instead.

How could good news feel so damn bad?

And how was she ever going to work up the courage to tell him?

"Are you planning on doing yoga or something?" Cam asked, a tease in his voice. "Because you've been on your knees on the floor now for at least fifteen minutes."

She lifted her head, giving him a wry look. "Maybe."

He grinned and reached a hand down to help her up.

"Listen," they both said at the same time, then laughed.

Since she was getting good at avoidance, she motioned for him to go first.

"If Darryl's up for watching a movie, I think we should bite the bullet and tell him we're dating," Cam said. "I'm tired of pretending like we're just friends." He moved closer, then gripped her upper arms. "Aren't you?"

She nodded. No matter what she still had to tell him, that wasn't a lie.

"After that, we can just let people figure it out. We don't need an engraved announcement."

"No." Her voice cracked. "No, we don't. But I…"

She trailed off, hating the words she had to say.

"What?"

"It's just that I don't really want to do movie night tonight."

"Oh. Okay."

"Oh, *fuck*." The word burst out of her, as harsh as cannon fire. She was such a damn coward.

"Mina? What—"

"I don't know how to tell you this," she blurted. "And if I don't spit it out, I'm never going to say it. I got a job in LA. An amazing freaking job. And I'm going to take it." She drew a breath as she glanced at his face, but she couldn't read a thing on it. His expression had gone completely blank.

"I see. Well, congratulations." His forehead creased and his lips moved, as if trying to form either words or a frown and not managing either. Then he walked toward the window, giving her his back.

She took a step toward him, but didn't go any closer. "Cam, please. Can't we talk about this?"

When he turned toward her, she saw the flash of anger before he smothered it, his features once again turning bland. "Sounds like the time for talking is past. From where I'm standing, this sounds like a done deal."

She said nothing.

His shoulders drooped. "How long have you known?"

"I got the call on Sunday when you were at The Fix. It's a big deal, Cam, them calling me on a Sunday. It's not a hire through Human Resources. I'm going to be a personal assistant to one of the studio's top execs."

"Fetching his coffee and picking up his dry cleaning. Sounds like exactly what you want."

"That's not fair."

"Probably not," he agreed, then cupped his hands on his head as he faced the floor. He looked back up again a moment later, his eyes narrow. "You knew before we went to Graffiti Park. You told Lydia before you told me."

She nodded.

"And you've already accepted?"

"It was too good to pass up."

He didn't respond to that. Instead, he asked, "And the job here? You're just blowing them off." He didn't say, *The way you're blowing me off*, but she heard it anyway.

"I'm going to go talk to them tomorrow morning. I want to tell them in person. I don't want to burn any bridges."

"No, you wouldn't want that."

"Cam," she began, but he cut her off with a sharp glance. She wished she could flip a switch and make him understand how amazing this was. This incredible job that she got on her own. Without her father or her brother or anyone pulling strings for her or stepping in as her safety net. Just her and her resume and the skill she brought to the table.

"How long before you go?"

Her stomach twisted. This felt like a job interview. Or a police interrogation.

"My plane leaves Wednesday morning."

She saw the impact of her words reflect on his face.

"You're blowing off The Fix? The contest? You're not even going to say hello to Kiki?"

"I didn't set the time frame," she protested.

"No, you didn't have anything to do with any of this."

She said nothing. His words were true, but they hurt.

He rubbed the bridge of his nose, then took a breath. And when he took a single step toward her, she felt her heart fill with hope. "Baby, why didn't you tell me?"

"Because they needed an answer right away. Because it's my dream job. Because I knew you wouldn't be happy for me. And because as much as I want the job, I don't want to leave you." She brushed away a tear, hating herself for crying.

His expression was gentle, but when he spoke the words sliced through her. "So your dream job has less responsibility than the one you have here?"

"You have no idea what responsibilities the job has."

"I may not work in your industry, but I'm not an idiot. And I know that dry cleaning and coffee isn't even close to an exaggeration. What happened to development? To being on the front lines?"

A hot wire of anger shot through her. "Don't tell me what job I want."

"I'm not. You're the one who's been telling me and Darryl for years. But you're not looking at the job. If you were, you'd see that you already had the dream job. You're just looking at the location."

"Hollywood? A studio job? Hell, yeah, I'm looking at the location. And you know what? You should, too."

"I should—what? What are you talking about?"

"You're laying this all at my feet, but you're not exactly tied to Austin. Kiki lives part time in LA, right? And you don't have a job yet. But you're making this all about me leaving you. Why don't we make it about you coming with me?"

It should have occurred to her before, but she'd been so wrapped up in the horror of leaving him that she hadn't thought it out. But it made perfect sense, and she told him so, relief flooding through her at having found a solution.

"And that's what you want?"

"Are you kidding? Of course. Do you think I want to lose you? It's perfect. I mean you could probably get a job at The Getty Center in a heartbeat."

"And the fact that I'm starting work on my doctorate in the fall?"

"There are universities in Los Angeles. Excellent ones with programs in rare books and manuscripts."

"And they'd probably even let me in. After I apply and wait a year. And what about my scholarship? It's not like I can afford UCLA or USC without one. Especially since I wouldn't have a job anymore."

Kiki would pay, she knew. But she also knew he'd never accept. Going through school on his own was important to Cam, just like getting to Hollywood was important to her. If she saw that about him, why couldn't he see it about her?

Frustrated, she sighed, then sat on the ottoman. "Well, then what do you want?"

It was a stupid thing to say, since she already knew the answer.

"I want you to stay here. I want you to work at the job you already accepted. The one that's going to give you so much hands-on responsibility. I want you to sit down with me and tell our families that we're dating. I want you in my bed every goddamn night. Hell, I just want to be with you, Mina. And I thought you wanted that, too."

"I do," she said, her voice so raw and hoarse she was afraid he couldn't even hear it. "I do, but I want LA, too."

"How exactly does that work, Mina? Because it seems to me that one cancels out the other."

"I don't know," she said, tasting the flood of tears she'd been fighting. "All I know is that I want you. But I also know that I have to go."

Chapter Fourteen

TUESDAY BROUGHT overcast skies and a generally yucky weather. Although that assessment might have had more to do with Mina's mood than actual meteorological conditions.

Even though she knew she needed to get out of bed and pack, Mina couldn't seem to manage anything more vigorous than thrusting her arm out every seven minutes to hit the snooze button, each time giving it a slightly harder whack.

After half an hour of that, she turned the alarm off entirely, then fell into a dreamless sleep and didn't wake up again until a crack of greenish light illuminated the room, followed by a deafening clap of thunder that shook the entire place.

She checked her clock, saw that it was already after six p.m., and tried to work up enough energy to even be frustrated with herself for sleeping through the entire damn day.

But no go. The day was gray, but her mood was grayer.

Usually, she loved Austin's frequent summer thunderstorms. They'd always seemed cozy before, as if inviting her to curl up on a couch with hot cocoa and a good book. Today, it just seemed depressing.

She didn't want to think about Cam or about leaving. And so, of course, that was all she was thinking about.

Cam didn't know a thing about the assistant position she'd taken, of course. So his dire predictions were nonsense. Sure, there'd be coffee and dry-cleaning. But she'd be making important connections in Hollywood, and that was key in the industry.

But even so, she'd called Griffin last night and asked him to make some phone calls to people he knew in Hollywood—just to make certain that her new boss didn't have a reputation for being an asshole who hit on women or abused his assistants or anything gnarly like that. Not that she was really worried. The job was exactly what she was looking for and she was sure her boss was a good guy.

Which begged the question of why she couldn't even get out of bed to start packing for the biggest adventure of her life.

The truth was, she didn't need to take much. She knew her dad would hire someone to pack and ship the rest of her things once she found an apartment in LA. But, of course, she still had to get up and get dressed, because she needed to go give the bad news to her new-and-soon-to-be-former Austin boss.

Except she didn't, because the day was gone.

She'd have to call tomorrow, after all.

She frowned, knowing that in-person would be better, but also relieved that she wouldn't see that look of disappointment on the team's faces—just like the expression she'd seen on Cam's.

Dammit, she wasn't supposed to be thinking of him.

That was the promise she'd made to herself last night. Today she had only one goal. Get ready to catch tomorrow morning's nine o'clock flight. That was it. Simple. Once she was on that plane, she'd have at least four hours to think about everything else before she landed. And Cam was at the top of her agenda.

Naturally, she blew that plan all to hell as thoughts of Cam filled her head when she finally peeled herself out of bed and made it into the shower.

The thing was, she loved him. She was certain of it. But if she stayed because of that, then she was making love a prison, and how could that be good? After all, her mom had loved her father, and when it fell apart, she was left with nothing.

Mina couldn't risk being like her mom. And if she stayed because Cam wanted her to—or even because she loved him—sooner or later, she'd resent him. And he'd feel the same if she begged him to move to LA, even though yesterday she'd shamelessly begged him to do just that.

So how did they work it out?

Was it even possible?

What she really wanted was to talk to Darryl, but she'd dug her own grave there by not clueing him in from the beginning.

Then again, what did she have to lose now? She'd already lost Cam—or she was in serious danger of it. And she'd sacrifice one hell of a lot more than her pride if she could figure out a way to get him back and make their lives mesh.

Her big brother had always been her savior before—and she'd always resented the hell out of it.

Now, as she thrust her arms in her light summer rain jacket, she desperately hoped that he'd put his arm around her, kiss her forehead, and make all the hurt go away.

***

"DARRYL!"

Mina wandered the rooms of her family home, realizing for the first time in her life that the place was ridiculously big for only three people. What had her father been thinking? And how the hell was she supposed to find anyone in these walls?

She scowled at the intercom button mounted near the entrance of every room, and wished that she and Darryl had been a little less rambunctious as kids. But they'd pushed that button with such abandon that her father had ultimately disconnected the entire system, vowing not to restore it until they were both adults.

Either he still considered them both children or he'd forgotten to get the system repaired.

Not that it mattered, the bottom line was that she couldn't find Darryl.

Since he'd started his clerkship, he'd left work promptly at five and come straight home. He'd told her this was the only law job that supported bankers' hours, and that his judge actually encouraged an eight-to-five schedule. So she expected him to be in the house.

But maybe he'd gone out for a drink with his co-clerks. Or grocery shopping. Or anywhere.

Which would make sense on any other day. But he knew this was her last night in town. So why wasn't he home to see her off?

Worried, she pulled her phone out and dialed him—which, actually, she should have thought of before, since calling or texting was a handy way of finding him in the house—but the phone went straight to voice mail all three times she tried.

"Fine," she muttered. "You want to be overprotective? I can, too."

Darryl had insisted they share their locations years ago. "You'll be walking around campus after dark," he'd said. "Don't be stupid."

She trusted him to not track her on a date, and she'd never looked up his location either, except for the one time he showed her how to do it.

Today, however, qualified as an emergency. And not just because he wasn't there the night before she left. No, a growing knot of worry had taken root in her stomach.

She didn't know if it was paranoia or a twin thing. But she was certain something bad had happened to him, and she stared at the phone screen, waiting for the little dot to place him somewhere.

When it did, she cringed.

Dell Seton Medical Hospital.

And although she couldn't know for sure, she was desperately afraid that the little red dot that represented Darryl was right smack dab in the emergency room.

Chapter Fifteen

"I WISH I HAD BETTER ADVICE," Kiki said, her voice sounding far away through the speaker of Cam's phone.

"That's okay," Cam assured her. He was in his too-soft bed leaning against the dingy gray co-op wall that matched his mood. "I shouldn't be calling you with personal stuff before you have to perform, anyway. I should have just waited until you get here tomorrow."

"From what you're telling me, she'll be in California by the time I make it down from Dallas."

"Yeah," he said, then put his forehead on his knees and sighed.

"Cam?"

"Just feeling sorry for myself. How do you and Noah handle it?"

"What? Our crazy careers? It's hard work, I won't lie. But we respect each other's goals, and at the end of the day we both know that the other comes first, before all the work stuff and everything else in the world. Even you, little brother."

He knew that was supposed to make him crack a smile, but all it did was twist his insides up again. "That's what I want," he told her. "That's how I feel."

"Is it?" she asked. "I don't see you packing up for LA."

Her words brought him up short. "You think I should?"

"No. But I'm also not saying that you shouldn't. You're the only one who can answer that."

He grimaced. "What the hell is the point of having an older sister if you don't boss me around?"

She laughed. "I don't know. To send you stupid text messages at least once a week and buy you lame Christmas presents?"

"Really? Damn. I thought there were more perks."

"Rough gig."

He smiled, then sighed as his thoughts invariably turned back to the Mina problem. "I guess I'm afraid it's one-sided. That I'll go, and I'll always be second to her career. That I'll always be the one making compromises."

"She's staring at her dream, Cam. You can't know right now what's truly important to her. Hell, she doesn't even know. But what you have to ask yourself is does it matter? You're pretty damn dedicated, too. Are you really going to pull out measuring sticks and try to figure out if you or work measures higher? How would you even tell?"

"Honestly, I don't know. All I know is that I want to wake up beside her. And I want to watch movies with her and roll my eyes at the way she criticizes the cinematography or the script. And I want to listen when she talks to herself while she's puttering around the house. I want a history with her, Kiki. And I think what I'm most afraid of is that her leaving means that she doesn't want one with me."

"Then you've answered your own question."

He stared at the phone. "I have?"

"Well, yeah, dummy. If that's the life you want, no way are you having it in Austin if she's moving to Los Angeles. So take a risk, get your ass to California, and figure out the answer for yourself."

THE FACT that Darryl was perfectly fine, with only a couple of abrasions on his calf and a mild concussion, did not ease any of Mina's fears or worries.

"I could have lost you," she said, for at least the hundredth time. "What the hell would I do without you?"

Just the thought made her want to curl up in a ball and moan. Losing Darryl. Losing Cameron. It was all too much to process, and she was compensating by going Mother Hen on him to the max.

As soon as they'd gotten back to the house, she'd made Darryl stretch out on the sofa in the living room with an ice pack on his head, a heating pad on his leg, and a big bowl of ice cream on a tray in front of him. "I'm okay," he protested again. "Although I'm happy to pretend to be an invalid if it gets me more ice cream."

"Do not even joke about this," she said sternly. "And what the hell were you doing cycling in the rain?"

"It wasn't raining when I went out after work. Just overcast."

"Even so," she said obstinately.

"Good point. I'll only bike when the sky is perfectly clear and little cartoon birdies follow me to provide any necessary assistance."

"Dammit, Darryl, a car hit you. You could have been killed. And why were you out with so little battery on your phone?"

She hadn't been able to reach him because his phone had run out of charge just moments after the driver who'd hit him had taken him to the ER to be checked out. Darryl had gotten his insurance information and assured the guy he was fine, then told him to go ahead and leave.

But he hadn't yet called Mina, and by the time he thought of it, his phone was dead and the driver was long gone. And while the nurses would have surely called, Darryl waited until after triage to ask them.

By that time, Mina had arrived.

"Obviously, I didn't realize it was so low on battery. But thank goodness for that last known location feature, right? I mean, technology." He held his hands out at his sides in a happy-go-lucky gesture. "Gotta love it, huh?"

"Stop joking about it." Tears trailed down her

cheeks, and his expression immediately shifted from amused irritation to concerned contrition.

"Oh, hell. I'm sorry I scared you," he said gently. "All he did was clip me on a corner. Yes, it could have been worse, but it wasn't. He could have just as easily hit a pedestrian. Come on, Mina. We both know there aren't guarantees."

"I know. I'm sorry. I'm just—" She sat at the foot of the couch, careful not to bump his leg, then grabbed a tissue from the coffee table and blew her nose.

"Just having a rough day overall?"

She sniffed, then looked up at him. "What do you mean?"

He tilted his head, as if considering how to answer. "Moving to LA. Leaving me. Leaving—you know—your friends. The internship at The Fix. All of that. It's gotta be hard."

Cam loomed in her mind, and she nodded. "It really is." She sucked in a breath. Time to bite the bullet. "Listen, I've been thinking about it, and I'm not—"

She stopped, her head turning toward the entry hall. She couldn't see the front door, but she distinctly heard the sound of someone punching in the unlock code.

Frowning, she met Darryl's eyes. "Dad?"

He shrugged, and she was just about to call out to their father when Cam's voice preceded him into the room. "*Darryl!* Do you have Mina's flight information? She's not home, and I need to get a ticket for tomorrow, and—*Oh*."

He looked between the two of them, as Mina stood

up and went to him, not even caring that Darryl was watching every move.

"Hey," she said. She expected a similar reply. Instead he took her face in his hands, held her steady, and kissed her so thoroughly that she thought her legs might melt.

When he finally released her, he glanced over at Darryl. "I'm dating your sister."

"Well, I hope so. Otherwise we need to enroll you in an etiquette refresher course. Because your greeting skills are a little over the top."

"What are you doing here?" Mina asked, still floating about ten feet off the ground.

"Coming to tell Darryl that I'm following you to LA. I'll find work somewhere—maybe The Getty—and I'll get my doctoral applications in as soon as I can. We'll make it work."

She took his hand, because if she didn't, she'd float even higher. She drew in air, as happy as she could ever remember being. "No," she said, "you're not."

"The hell I'm not. I've been thinking about this—"

"I'm staying here," she said, effectively cutting him off.

"What? Why?"

She pulled him over to the couch. There wasn't much room, but that was okay, since Mina was mostly sitting on Cam's lap.

"What happened to you?" Cam said, peering at Darryl, and apparently only now noticing his invalid state.

"A car ran me over," Darryl said dismissively. "Who cares? I want to know why she's staying."

"Fair enough," Cam said. "Not that I'm arguing, but why?"

"Because I don't want to lose you," she said, feeling his reaction to her words in the way his grip tightened, pulling her even closer. "Because I don't want you to have to sacrifice even a year of your education so I can chase a dream in LA when I could chase the same dream in Austin."

"You don't want to move to LA?"

"Oh, sometime, yes. But right now, this is home. You, Darryl, our friends." She lifted a shoulder. "I have a life here, and I want to build onto it. With you," she said, then brushed a kiss over his lips. "And when you're done with school," she added lightly, "I'll expect you to look for jobs in Southern California."

He laughed. "Fair enough."

"Were you really going to move out there for me?" she asked.

"There's not much I wouldn't do for you."

"This is all very heartwarming," Darryl said. "But what about the stellar job out there? Are you just going to turn it down?"

"I already did," she said. "I sent an email from the ER." She lifted a shoulder, then met Cam's eyes. "I never did decline the job offer here. His accident distracted me. And it's a much better opportunity anyway. Lots of hands-on experience. And that exec in

LA is probably lame like you said. Coffee and dry-cleaning and then he tosses you out and drags in a new PA. Not even worth my time."

"Except you know he's not," Cam said, and her heart picked up tempo. She'd learned the truth from Griffin just a few hours ago. But how the hell had Cam?

"He really is a stellar exec," Cam continued. "Yes, the job is a lot of fetching coffee—I was right about that —but his former assistants have gone on to write scripts, produce movies, create television shows."

His brow furrowed, and she felt her eyes prick with tears. "You're walking away from all that? You're sure?"

She leaned forward and kissed him. "Yeah," she said. "I'm sure. I'll still end up in Hollywood. I'll get there with a great resume full of real experiences and not coffee and dry-cleaning. And I'll make contacts from Austin, too. And when I do go to California, I won't be alone. I'm absolutely positive." She drew in a shuddering breath. "I love you, Cameron Reed."

"Oh, baby. I love you, too."

"How did you know about the exec?" she asked.

"Griffin told me. Said you wanted to know what the buzz was about him. Then he said that if he was in my place, he'd want to know that it was a good job and you'd make great connections."

"But—wait. I don't get it. Why would he even think to tell you?"

"Probably because I told him you two were dating," Darryl said.

Mina gaped. "Wait. What?"

"Well, it came up. I was chatting with him about the work you did for him. He thinks you'll go far in the biz, by the way."

"Came up? But how did you know we were dating in the first place?"

He pointed to his head. "Slightly concussed," he said. "But not blind. I've known for ages. Why do you think Zach blew off my party? I might have told him you two were involved, and the twerp wasn't interested enough in just coming to celebrate me."

"And you don't mind?" Cam asked. "It's not weird?"

"You're both weird. You're also two of my favorite people. Now I don't have to worry about either one of you hooking up with a loser." He looked between the two of them. "Just lock your doors if you're having sex, okay? My eyes are still burning."

"Asshole!" Mina said, then threw a pillow at him.

"Love you, Meanie," he said, holding up his fingers in the *I Love You*, sign.

"Love you back, Dickbreath," she said, returning the sign.

Darryl snorted. "So is it safe to assume that you two have made up now?"

Mina looked at Cam, who nodded. "Oh, yeah," he said.

"Definitely," Mina agreed.

"Good. Then go have wild make up sex, okay?" He grabbed the remote off the coffee table. "There's a show starting that I really want to watch."

And since Mina couldn't argue with that, she stood

up, took Cameron's hand, and led him back to her apartment.

Chapter Sixteen

CAM'S EYES locked on Mina's as he filled her, taking his time as he thrust slow and deep, wanting to make this last. Hell, wanting it to never end.

She was his. And, yes, he was hers. Fully. Completely. And with a lifetime of adventures spread out in front of him.

He still couldn't quite believe that she was staying— much less that she was staying for him. But then he looked deep in her eyes again and saw the love reflected there, and knew that it was true.

"Come with me," he whispered, the passion in his mind filtering down to his body. He had to claim her now. Had to see that same joy and release on her face that he felt in himself.

She nodded, her lips parted, her breath coming ragged. "I love you," she whispered, and that was the final straw—the intimate touch of her voice that pushed him over the edge, and he lost all control as he exploded inside her, his climax triggering hers, so that she went over when he did, her core tightening around him, her muscles drawing him further in as her fingernails dug into his back, pulling him closer and closer, as if at any moment they would become one person.

When the explosion settled and he felt whole again, he rolled next to her, exhausted, then took her hand. "I love you," he whispered, because he really couldn't say it enough.

"I know," she said. "I love you, too." She sighed, then sat up. "I have something for you."

"Yeah?"

He watched as she got out of bed, then went naked to her dresser. She opened a drawer and pointed to it. "I emptied it out. It's yours. I figure you can leave some stuff here. For when you sleep here instead of that ratty co-op."

He sat up, amused. "This entire huge apartment, and I only get a drawer?"

Her brows lifted. "Wouldn't want to move too fast."

"We've known each other our whole lives, Mina," he teased. "There's no *too fast* in this equation."

She came back to the bed and sat beside him, her hand sliding down to cup his cock. "Good point. Prove your worth, and I'll clear out some space in my closet, too."

Laughing, he tumbled her onto the bed, then got on top of her. "I can do that," he said, then kissed her lightly. "And by the way," he added, as she writhed naked beneath him. "I really do love my drawer."

CAM STOOD in the office at The Fix on Wednesday afternoon going over details with Nolan, Tyree, Brooke, and Jenna. "I just want to make sure it's okay if Nolan puts my bit during the contest on *Mornings With Wood*." He glanced at Brooke. "There's not any sort of conflict with your show, is there?"

She shook her head. "None at all. I double-checked with the producers after Nolan mentioned maybe doing promo spots for the bar during his show. It's all good."

"And the more publicity for the bar, the better," Jenna added.

"Amen to that," Tyree said.

"Speaking of," Cam continued, "Kiki checked with her manager and so long as you sign all the forms he's emailing over, then you can also broadcast snippets of her performance. You too," he added to Nolan, who rubbed his hands together in glee. "In fact, she and Noah should be here any minute."

"I guess that makes our timing perfect," Kiki said, coming into the office and making a beeline for Cameron. "God, I've missed you," she said, pulling him into a tight hug.

She gave him one more squeeze, then swooped into Tyree's arms as well. "It's been ages since I saw you. I'm so glad this worked out. Oh! I forgot introductions."

She turned to indicate the men in the doorway. Cam knew his brother-in-law, Noah, of course. And Noah stood beside another man who Cam had met once or twice. A billionaire several times over, Damien Stark was a former tennis champion turned entrepreneur, with enough money and scandal in his background to keep him and his wife, Nikki, on pretty much constant display in the tabloids.

"Tyree, you already know my husband, Noah," Kiki said, then introduced Noah around the room. "And this is his boss—"

"And friend," Stark put in.

Kiki laughed and nodded in acknowledgement. "And friend," she agreed. "Damien Stark."

"It's a pleasure to be here," Stark said, leaning against the doorframe and looking as if he owned the place. All things considered, Cam figured that if Stark wanted to, he could probably write a check.

Then again, maybe not. Cam knew damn well that Tyree had no intention of selling. That was the whole point of the calendar contest and the other ramped up promo. To keep the place in the black—and in Tyree and his partners' hands.

"I'm impressed with everything you've rolled out with an eye toward increasing revenues," Stark said. "And I'm definitely looking forward to the calendar contest tonight. I understand you put on quite a show last time," he added, with a wry glance toward Cam.

"Anything for my adoring public," Cam quipped, as Kiki rolled her eyes and the others laughed.

"Forgive my brother. He's an idiot. I saw Mina on my way in, by the way. She said I was supposed to give you this," she added to Cam, then blew him a kiss. Silly, but Cam caught it, warmed by the knowledge that Mina was just beyond those walls thinking of him.

"I don't suppose you have any more ideas for The Fix," Tyree asked Stark. "You built an empire from the ground up. Any tips you want to toss my way…"

Stark probably got asked that kind of question a hundred times each day. But if he was irritated, he didn't show it. On the contrary, he ticked off the various things that the bar had already implemented to increase the customer base and, therefore, the revenue. And it really was a nice, long list.

"To be honest, I don't have a thing to add," Stark said with what sounded like genuine approval.

"Whoa," Tyree said. "I was just looking for an off-the-cuff answer. I didn't realize you'd taken the time to look into what we're doing here. Thank you, man."

Stark nodded toward Kiki, who shrugged. "What can I say? I was in marketing for years and Damien speaks the language. We talked."

"All kidding aside," Stark said, "I think that short of a collection plate, you're doing what needs to be done. And if you *are* taking donations, I'd be happy to contribute."

Tyree shook his head. "This bar earns its right to keep the doors open, or it doesn't keep them open."

"I speak his language, too," Damien said, nodding with approval toward Tyree.

"Actually, there is one thing you could help with," Jenna said, stepping forward and looking just a tiny bit intimidated.

"What's that?"

"Enter the contest," Brooke interrupted, laughing. "You'd be a big hit."

"My wife might be less than thrilled."

"Is Nikki here?" Kiki asked.

He shook his head. "She was hoping to fly out to see you perform, but she texted me this morning that our nanny's ill. She's hoping to find a friend to watch the girls, but it doesn't sound likely."

"Too bad. I haven't seen her in ages," Kiki said, then turned to Jenna whose hand had moved to her belly at the talk of kids. "Sorry. We derailed you. What were you going to suggest?"

"Well, it turns out that Beverly's under the weather, too. She said she'll come do it if we can't find someone else. But it occurred to me that Mr. Stark would be a great replacement."

For the first time, Stark looked a little out of his element. He turned, taking in all the faces—each of whom seemed enthusiastic about the plan. "Ah, I hate to ask. But replacement for what, exactly?"

SINCE CAMERON WAS ACTUALLY ENTERED in the Man of the Month contest, Brooke and Spencer told

Mina that not only did she not have to work, she wasn't allowed to. So instead of running a camera, she had a table front and center with Darryl and Noah Carter and Damien Stark.

Not bad company, even if she was so intimidated by Damien and Noah that she was finding it hard to make conversation now that Kiki had left their table to go on stage to thunderous applause.

She was followed by Tyree, who grinned broadly as he reached out to the crowd, thanking them for coming and telling them he hoped they would enjoyed the surprise performance before the Man of the Month contest began.

"And it's a double surprise. Those of you who've been coming for the last few contests, probably expected to see Beverly Martin up here as our emcee. Well, unfortunately, Bev's a little under the weather." He paused for the sounds of sympathy. "But don't worry, you have a rock solid replacement. And, no, it's not me."

This time, he paused for the titters of laughter, and Mina had to admit she was impressed with the way Tyree handled a crowd. She knew he'd led men in the military, but leading an audience was entirely different.

"Ladies and gentlemen, please welcome a man who I hope needs no introduction, because I'm damn sure not reading his novel-length resume, Mr. Damien Stark."

Taylor was working the spotlight, and Mina saw her shift it to find Damien at their table. He waved to the crowd, illuminated more by the flashes of camera phones than from the huge spotlight itself.

He made his way to the stage, not the least bit fazed by all the hubbub. He stood for a moment, his hands up in a useless attempt to quell the chatter. Finally, he just picked up the microphone and began talking.

"Welcome to The Fix, everyone. I'm Damien Stark, and I'll be your emcee this evening." He paused just long enough for applause, then started back in, introducing Kiki and telling the audience about how she'd performed on that very stage before her band, Pink Chameleon, got back together. "And a good thing they did or we'd all have missed out on some incredible, award winning songs.

"I understand the band is performing in San Antonio tomorrow, but we have a special treat, because Kiki is going to perform a new song that hasn't made it into their repertoire. Ladies and gentlemen, Kiki King."

Mina was awed by how smooth he was with no rehearsal, but then she was blown away as she watched Kiki. She'd known Cam's sister almost her whole life, but the age difference was such that they didn't hang out together. In fact, most of their contact was when Kiki had babysat her.

Now, Kiki sat on that stool with nothing but a guitar, and brought the audience to tears with the love song that she sang to the room, but turned back to Noah for the refrain.

"You're everything right, you're everything wrong

You're the point of this song
The man who knows me, the man who sees
Darling, please
Don't you ever stop loving me."

Beside Mina, Darryl whispered, "Wow," and across the table, Noah sat enraptured. Mina felt the same way, and she twisted in her seat to find Cam, but he was in the back bar with the other contestants, watching the show from the doorway. She saw a glimpse of his hair, but that was all.

It was enough to make her crave him, though, and as Kiki left the stage to enthusiastic applause, Mina sighed, wishing that she had the ability to voice her emotions that way.

When Stark returned to the stage, she could see real emotion in his face as he found Kiki at their table and tilted his head in approval. "Now my wife is really going to be upset she mi—" He stopped, his eyes going to someone off stage near the main door to the bar. Mina caught Noah's eyes, who shrugged, but stood up to peer over the crowd as Darryl did the same on the other side of Mina.

Too short, Mina couldn't manage, but she could tell from Noah's amused grin and the look of undiluted love on Stark's face that Nikki Fairchild Stark must have made it after all.

For a beat, Damien simply looked at her. "Mrs. Stark," he finally said, as he pointed to his vacant chair at Mina's table. "Your seat."

Mina had heard the scandal story about Stark offering the former Texas beauty queen a million dollars in exchange for a nude portrait. Maybe that really was how it started between them, and maybe it wasn't, but as Nikki came closer, it only took one look at the two of them for Mina to know there was nothing contrived or fake about their commitment.

"And I think that's plenty for the warm-up," Stark said, laughing. "Now it's time for the real show."

After she was seated, Nikki explained to Noah and Kiki that she'd found a sitter. "Thank goodness for Grayson," she added. "I hate using one of the jets just for me, but I didn't want to miss your performance. You've been on the road so much we haven't talked in ages." She turned to Darryl and Mina, then flashed a wide, sincere smile. "I'm Nikki."

Mina laughed. "Believe me, I know," she said, then realized how horrible that sounded. Nikki, however just nodded toward the stage with a wry grin. "The price I pay for being married to him. Everybody knows me."

That was probably true, Mina assumed, but from what she could tell, Nikki thought he price was more than fair.

"I'm Darryl, and this is my sister Mina. Glad you could make it."

"Mina's Cam's girlfriend," Kiki explained.

"Oh! He's competing, isn't he? This should be fun."

Kiki rolled her eyes and Mina soaked up the solidarity, enjoying the company, Damien's easy banter, and the first eleven men who strolled across the stage.

"Saving the best for last," she said to the table at large.

Damien's voice boomed out, "Please welcome the final contestant for Mr. March, Cameron Reed."

Cam strolled up the red carpet looking as comfortable as if he was at home. He wore jeans and, Mina noticed, one of his button down shirts that she'd claimed as her own to sleep in since it was missing some buttons and the cuffs were frayed. Not what she would have picked for an onstage experience, but she supposed he had his reasons.

Nolan crouched at the base of the stage, his microphone on a stand and a handheld camera in his hand. She'd have to remember to check his Facebook page later tonight.

"Ladies, I know I'm supposed to say something to convince you to vote for me for Mr. March. But the truth is, I only have one thing to say and one woman to say it to."

Oh no.

Darryl nudged her as everyone else at their table turned her direction, and as they did—as Nolan pointed his camera right at her—she felt her cheeks flush.

Cam thrust his hand out, his finger pointing at her as his hips did a Chippendale's style swivel that had her cheeks heating even more. "You're mine, Mina Silver. And," he added as he ripped open the shirt to reveal his almost bare abs, "I'm yours."

Sure enough, there was another message scrawled in lipstick on his chest. This time, it said, "Mina's."

"Yes, you are!" she called out as she jumped to her feet, making the audience howl and applaud.

Then the music started, he strolled off, and Darryl smacked the table with unrestrained laughter.

She was still giddy when she threw herself into his arms five minutes later. He was shirtless, all the men were, and she got lipstick all over her blouse. Not that she cared. "I love you," she said.

After a moment, she pulled gently away. "I brought you a present."

"Really?" He looked surprised, but pleased.

She grabbed her purse, then handed him the flat object wrapped in tissue. "It was a last-minute wrapping job," she said apologetically.

As soon as he unwrapped it, and she saw the tender awe on his face, she knew she didn't need to apologize. He pulled out the framed photo of his graffiti art—*Mina + Cam 4ever*.

"I wanted to memorialize it," she said. "Now even if they do demolish the park, at least we really will be forever.

"Do you have any idea how much I love you?" he asked.

"Tell me."

He looked around, as if trying to find the right words. Then he nodded toward the stage where Nikki and Damien stood talking close together, the love on their faces so vibrant it was humbling.

"Those two? They don't have anything on our love," Cam said.

She lifted her eyes to his, losing herself in humor and passion. "No competition at all," she agreed, then melted into in the arms of the man who was her past and her future, who knew her fears and her dreams. With Cameron, the future was safe, because whatever came next, she knew they'd handle it together.

Epilogue

SHELBY DRAKE WATCHED as Nolan stood on stage next to the newly crowned Mr. March, Cameron Reed, and told his radio audience that Cameron not only had big sparkly balls, he also had fine taste in women.

In the audience, the dark-haired girl that Cameron had singled out during the contest blushed again, and Shelby knew there was something between her and Cameron. But that's about all Shelby knew. Mostly because she hadn't been paying attention to the Mr. March contest at all.

She'd come to The Fix tonight for one reason, and one reason only—to make a new play in the battle of wills that had been going on between her and Nolan for weeks.

She pressed her legs together under the small table, remembering all the wicked things he'd done to her. The kind of things that she'd never imagined doing in a million years, but couldn't deny that she liked.

She knew that he believed he had the upper hand. That he thought she would never manage to surprise him.

Well, tonight she was just drunk enough to try.

Before she could talk herself out of it, she scribbled a note on the back of her receipt, then folded it over three times and added a twenty as a tip before handing it to the waitress she'd called over. "Make sure Nolan gets that when he comes off the stage, please. And if you would, tell him to read it right away. It's important."

"Sure," the girl said, then hurried away to take care of another customer in the jam-packed bar.

Shelby stood, knowing she was going to lose her table, but that was okay. She had only one more thing to do, and then she was leaving.

A little wobbly on the unfamiliar heels, she hurried to the back, then waited for a free stall to open up in the ladies room. She didn't need to use the facilities; she only needed privacy, and she emerged in less than five minutes, the wobbly feeling now upgraded to exposed and decadent and decidedly naughty.

She left the restroom, certain that all eyes were on her. That everyone in the place knew what she was doing. That they were all staring down her cleavage, now revealed by the fact that she'd opened the top four buttons of her silk blouse, revealing the lacy trim of her camisole.

As she'd hoped, Nolan had read the note, and he was waiting for her at the end of the bar, his expression concerned. "Shel? What is it?" His eyes dipped to her neckline, and she saw the confusion in his eyes and the furrow of his brow. "Are you okay?"

"I'm fine," she said. "I have something for you." Then she reached into her purse and put the small ball of crumpled material into his hand.

After that, she drew in a breath and hurried past him toward the door, forcing herself not to look back to see if Nolan was following, or if he was still standing in the middle of The Fix, her red *La Perla* panties held tight in his hand.

Yeah, she thought. *Game on.*

The Men of Man of the Month!

Are you eager to learn which Man of the Month book features which sexy hero? Here's a handy list!

Down On Me - meet Reece
Hold On Tight - meet Spencer
Need You Now - meet Cameron
Start Me Up - meet Nolan
Get It On - meet Tyree
In Your Eyes - meet Parker
Turn Me On - meet Derek
Shake It Up - meet Landon
All Night Long - meet Easton
In Too Deep - meet Matthew
Light My Fire - meet Griffin
Walk The Line - meet Brent
&
Bar Bites: A Man of the Month Cookbook

Down On Me excerpt

Did you miss book one in the Man of the Month series? Here's an excerpt from Down On Me!

Chapter One

Reece Walker ran his palms over the slick, soapy ass of the woman in his arms and knew that he was going straight to hell.

Not because he'd slept with a woman he barely knew. Not because he'd enticed her into bed with a series of well-timed bourbons and particularly inventive half-truths. Not even because he'd lied to his best friend Brent about why Reece couldn't drive with him to the airport to pick up Jenna, the third player in their trifecta of lifelong friendship.

No, Reece was staring at the fiery pit because he was a lame, horny asshole without the balls to tell the naked beauty standing in the shower with him that she wasn't the woman he'd been thinking about for the last four hours.

And if that wasn't one of the pathways to hell, it damn sure ought to be.

He let out a sigh of frustration, and Megan tilted her head, one eyebrow rising in question as she slid her hand down to stroke his cock, which was demonstrating no guilt whatsoever about the whole going to hell issue. "Am I boring you?"

"Hardly." That, at least, was the truth. He felt like a prick, yes. But he was a well-satisfied one. "I was just thinking that you're beautiful."

She smiled, looking both shy and pleased—and Reece felt even more like a heel. What the devil was wrong with him? She *was* beautiful. And hot and funny and easy to talk to. Not to mention good in bed.

But she wasn't Jenna, which was a ridiculous comparison. Because Megan qualified as fair game, whereas Jenna was one of his two best friends. She trusted him. Loved him. And despite the way his cock perked up at the thought of doing all sorts of delicious things with her in bed, Reece knew damn well that would never happen. No way was he risking their friendship. Besides, Jenna didn't love him like that. Never had, never would.

And that—plus about a billion more reasons—meant that Jenna was entirely off-limits.

Too bad his vivid imagination hadn't yet gotten the memo.

Fuck it.

He tightened his grip, squeezing Megan's perfect rear. "Forget the shower," he murmured. "I'm taking you back to bed." He needed this. Wild. Hot. Demanding. And dirty enough to keep him from thinking.

Hell, he'd scorch the earth if that's what it took to burn Jenna from his mind—and he'd leave Megan limp, whimpering, and very, very satisfied. His guilt. Her pleasure. At least it would be a win for one of them.

And who knows? Maybe he'd manage to fuck the fantasies of his best friend right out of his head.

It didn't work.

Reece sprawled on his back, eyes closed, as Megan's gentle fingers traced the intricate outline of the tattoos inked across his pecs and down his arms. Her touch was warm and tender, in stark contrast to the way he'd just fucked her—a little too wild, a little too hard, as if he were fighting a battle, not making love.

Well, that was true, wasn't it?

But it was a battle he'd lost. Victory would have brought oblivion. Yet here he was, a naked woman beside him, and his thoughts still on Jenna, as wild and intense and impossible as they'd been since that night eight months ago when the earth had shifted beneath him, and he'd let himself look at her as a woman and not as a friend.

One breathtaking, transformative night, and Jenna

didn't even realize it. And he'd be damned if he'd ever let her figure it out.

Beside him, Megan continued her exploration, one fingertip tracing the outline of a star. "No names? No wife or girlfriend's initials hidden in the design?"

He turned his head sharply, and she burst out laughing.

"Oh, don't look at me like that." She pulled the sheet up to cover her breasts as she rose to her knees beside him. "I'm just making conversation. No hidden agenda at all. Believe me, the last thing I'm interested in is a relationship." She scooted away, then sat on the edge of the bed, giving him an enticing view of her bare back. "I don't even do overnights."

As if to prove her point, she bent over, grabbed her bra off the floor, and started getting dressed.

"Then that's one more thing we have in common." He pushed himself up, rested his back against the head-board, and enjoyed the view as she wiggled into her jeans.

"Good," she said, with such force that he knew she meant it, and for a moment he wondered what had soured her on relationships.

As for himself, he hadn't soured so much as fizzled. He'd had a few serious girlfriends over the years, but it never worked out. No matter how good it started, invariably the relationship crumbled. Eventually, he had to acknowledge that he simply wasn't relationship material. But that didn't mean he was a monk, the last eight months notwithstanding.

She put on her blouse and glanced around, then slipped her feet into her shoes. Taking the hint, he got up and pulled on his jeans and T-shirt. "Yes?" he asked, noticing the way she was eying him speculatively.

"The truth is, I was starting to think you might be in a relationship."

"What? Why?"

She shrugged. "You were so quiet there for a while, I wondered if maybe I'd misjudged you. I thought you might be married and feeling guilty."

Guilty.

The word rattled around in his head, and he groaned. "Yeah, you could say that."

"Oh, *hell.* Seriously?"

"No," he said hurriedly. "Not that. I'm not cheating on my non-existent wife. I wouldn't. Not ever." Not in small part because Reece wouldn't ever have a wife since he thought the institution of marriage was a crock, but he didn't see the need to explain that to Megan.

"But as for guilt?" he continued. "Yeah, tonight I've got that in spades."

She relaxed slightly. "Hmm. Well, sorry about the guilt, but I'm glad about the rest. I have rules, and I consider myself a good judge of character. It makes me cranky when I'm wrong."

"Wouldn't want to make you cranky."

"Oh, you really wouldn't. I can be a total bitch." She sat on the edge of the bed and watched as he tugged on his boots. "But if you're not hiding a wife in your attic, what are you feeling guilty about? I assure you, if it has anything to do with my satisfaction, you needn't feel guilty at all." She flashed a mischievous grin, and he couldn't help but smile back. He hadn't invited a woman into his bed for eight long months. At least he'd had the good fortune to pick one he actually liked.

"It's just that I'm a crappy friend," he admitted.

"I doubt that's true."

"Oh, it is," he assured her as he tucked his wallet into his back pocket. The irony, of course, was that as far as Jenna knew, he was an excellent friend. The best. One of her two pseudo-brothers with whom she'd sworn a blood oath the summer after sixth grade, almost twenty years ago.

From Jenna's perspective, Reece was at least as good as Brent, even if the latter scored bonus points because he was picking Jenna up at the airport while Reece was trying to fuck his personal demons into oblivion. Trying anything, in fact, that would exorcise the memory of how she'd clung to him that night, her curves enticing and her breath intoxicating, and not just because of the scent of too much alcohol.

She'd trusted him to be the white knight, her noble rescuer, and all he'd been able to think about was the feel of her body, soft and warm against his, as he carried her up the stairs to her apartment.

A wild craving had hit him that night, like a tidal wave of emotion crashing over him, washing away the outer shell of friendship and leaving nothing but raw desire and a longing so potent it nearly brought him to his knees.

It had taken all his strength to keep his distance when the only thing he'd wanted was to cover every inch of her naked body with kisses. To stroke her skin and watch her writhe with pleasure.

He'd won a hard-fought battle when he reined in his desire that night. But his victory wasn't without its wounds. She'd pierced his heart when she'd drifted to sleep in his arms, whispering that she loved him—and he knew that she meant it only as a friend.

More than that, he knew that he was the biggest asshole to ever walk the earth.

Thankfully, Jenna remembered nothing of that night. The liquor had stolen her memories, leaving her with a monster hangover, and him with a Jenna-shaped hole in his heart.

"Well?" Megan pressed. "Are you going to tell me? Or do I have to guess?"

"I blew off a friend."

"Yeah? That probably won't score you points in the Friend of the Year competition, but it doesn't sound too dire. Unless you were the best man and blew off the wedding? Left someone stranded at the side of the road somewhere in West Texas? Or promised to feed their cat and totally forgot? Oh, God. Please tell me you didn't kill Fluffy."

He bit back a laugh, feeling slightly better. "A friend came in tonight, and I feel like a complete shit for not meeting her plane."

"Well, there are taxis. And I assume she's an adult?"

"She is, and another friend is there to pick her up."

"I see," she said, and the way she slowly nodded suggested that she saw too much. "I'm guessing that *friend* means *girlfriend*? Or, no. You wouldn't do that. So she must be an ex."

"Really not," he assured her. "Just a friend. Lifelong, since sixth grade."

"Oh, I get it. Longtime friend. High expectations. She's going to be pissed."

"Nah. She's cool. Besides, she knows I usually work nights."

"Then what's the problem?"

He ran his hand over his shaved head, the bristles from the day's growth like sandpaper against his palm. "Hell if I know," he lied, then forced a smile, because whether his problem was guilt or lust or just plain stupidity, she hardly deserved to be on the receiving end of his bullshit.

He rattled his car keys. "How about I buy you one last drink before I take you home?"

"You're sure you don't mind a working drink?" Reece asked as he helped Megan out of his cherished baby blue vintage Chevy pickup. "Normally I wouldn't take you to my job, but we just hired a new bar back, and I want to see how it's going."

He'd snagged one of the coveted parking spots on Sixth Street, about a block down from The Fix, and he glanced automatically toward the bar, the glow from the windows relaxing him. He didn't own the place, but it was like a second home to him and had been for one hell of a long time.

"There's a new guy in training, and you're not there? I thought you told me you were the manager?"

"I did, and I am, but Tyree's there. The owner, I mean. He's always on site when someone new is starting. Says it's his job, not mine. Besides, Sunday's my day off, and Tyree's a stickler for keeping to the schedule."

"Okay, but why are you going then?"

"Honestly? The new guy's my cousin. He'll probably give me shit for checking in on him, but old habits die hard." Michael had been almost four when Vincent died, and the loss of his dad hit him hard. At sixteen, Reece had tried to be stoic, but Uncle Vincent had been like a second father to him, and he'd always thought of Mike as more brother than cousin. Either way, from that day on, he'd made it his job to watch out for the kid.

"Nah, he'll appreciate it," Megan said. "I've got a little sister, and she gripes when I check up on her, but it's all for show. She likes knowing I have her back. And as for getting a drink where you work, I don't mind at all."

As a general rule, late nights on Sunday were dead, both in the bar and on Sixth Street, the popular downtown Austin street that had been a focal point of the city's nightlife for decades. Tonight was no exception. At half-past one in the morning, the street was mostly deserted. Just a few cars moving slowly, their headlights shining toward the west, and a smattering of couples, stumbling and laughing. Probably tourists on their way back to one of the downtown hotels.

It was late April, though, and the spring weather was drawing both locals and tourists. Soon, the area—and the bar—would be bursting at the seams. Even on a slow Sunday night.

Situated just a few blocks down from Congress Avenue, the main downtown artery, The Fix on Sixth attracted a healthy mix of tourists and locals. The bar had existed in one form or another for decades, becoming a local staple, albeit one that had been falling deeper and deeper into disrepair until Tyree had bought the place six years ago and started it on much-needed life support.

"You've never been here before?" Reece asked as he paused in front of the oak and glass doors etched with the bar's familiar logo.

"I only moved downtown last month. I was in Los Angeles before."

The words hit Reece with unexpected force. Jenna had been in LA, and a wave of both longing and regret crashed over him. He should have gone with Brent. What the hell kind of friend was he, punishing Jenna because he couldn't control his own damn libido?

With effort, he forced the thoughts back. He'd already beaten that horse to death.

"Come on," he said, sliding one arm around her shoulder and pulling open the door with his other. "You're going to love it."

He led her inside, breathing in the familiar mix of

alcohol, southern cooking, and something indiscernible he liked to think of as the scent of a damn good time. As he expected, the place was mostly empty. There was no live music on Sunday nights, and at less than an hour to closing, there were only three customers in the front room.

"Megan, meet Cameron," Reece said, pulling out a stool for her as he nodded to the bartender in introduction. Down the bar, he saw Griffin Draper, a regular, lift his head, his face obscured by his hoodie, but his attention on Megan as she chatted with Cam about the house wines.

Reece nodded hello, but Griffin turned back to his notebook so smoothly and nonchalantly that Reece wondered if maybe he'd just been staring into space, thinking, and hadn't seen Reece or Megan at all. That was probably the case, actually. Griff wrote a popular podcast that had been turned into an even more popular web series, and when he wasn't recording the dialogue, he was usually writing a script.

"So where's Mike? With Tyree?"

Cameron made a face, looking younger than his twenty-four years. "Tyree's gone."

"You're kidding. Did something happen with Mike?" His cousin was a responsible kid. Surely he hadn't somehow screwed up his first day on the job.

"No, Mike's great." Cam slid a Scotch in front of Reece. "Sharp, quick, hard worker. He went off the clock about an hour ago, though. So you just missed him."

"Tyree shortened his shift?"

Cam shrugged. "Guess so. Was he supposed to be on until closing?"

"Yeah." Reece frowned. "He was. Tyree say why he cut him loose?"

"No, but don't sweat it. Your cousin's fitting right in. Probably just because it's Sunday and slow. " He made a face. "And since Tyree followed him out, guess who's closing for the first time alone."

"So you're in the hot seat, huh? " Reece tried to sound casual. He was standing behind Megan's stool, but now he moved to lean against the bar, hoping his casual posture suggested that he wasn't worried at all. He was, but he didn't want Cam to realize it. Tyree didn't leave employees to close on their own. Not until he'd spent weeks training them.

"I told him I want the weekend assistant manager position. I'm guessing this is his way of seeing how I work under pressure."

"Probably," Reece agreed half-heartedly. "What did he say?"

"Honestly, not much. He took a call in the office, told Mike he could head home, then about fifteen minutes later said he needed to take off, too, and that I was the man for the night."

"Trouble?" Megan asked.

"No. Just chatting up my boy," Reece said, surprised at how casual his voice sounded. Because the scenario had trouble printed all over it. He just wasn't sure what kind of trouble.

He focused again on Cam. "What about the wait-staff?" Normally, Tiffany would be in the main bar taking care of the customers who sat at tables. "He didn't send them home, too, did he?"

"Oh, no," Cam said. "Tiffany and Aly are scheduled to be on until closing, and they're in the back with—"

But his last words were drowned out by a high-pitched squeal of "*You're here!*" and Reece looked up to find Jenna Montgomery—the woman he craved—barreling across the room and flinging herself into his arms.

Meet Damien Stark

Only his passion could set her free…

Release Me
Claim Me
Complete Me
Anchor Me
Lost With Me

Meet Damien Stark in Release Me, *book 1 of the wildly sensual series that's left millions of readers breathless …*

Chapter One

A cool ocean breeze caresses my bare shoulders, and I shiver, wishing I'd taken my roommate's advice and brought a shawl with me tonight. I arrived in Los Angeles only four days ago, and I haven't yet adjusted to the concept of summer temperatures changing with the setting of the sun. In Dallas, June is hot, July is hotter, and August is hell.

Not so in California, at least not by the beach. LA Lesson Number One: Always carry a sweater if you'll be out after dark.

Of course, I could leave the balcony and go back inside to the party. Mingle with the millionaires. Chat up the celebrities. Gaze dutifully at the paintings. It is a gala art opening, after all, and my boss brought me here to meet and greet and charm and chat. Not to lust over the panorama that is coming alive in front of me. Bloodred clouds bursting against the pale orange sky. Blue-gray waves shimmering with dappled gold.

I press my hands against the balcony rail and lean forward, drawn to the intense, unreachable beauty of the setting sun. I regret that I didn't bring the battered Nikon I've had since high school. Not that it would have fit in my itty-bitty beaded purse. And a bulky camera bag paired with a little black dress is a big, fat fashion no-no.

But this is my very first Pacific Ocean sunset, and I'm determined to document the moment. I pull out my iPhone and snap a picture.

"Almost makes the paintings inside seem redundant, doesn't it?" I recognize the throaty, feminine voice and turn to face Evelyn Dodge, retired actress turned agent turned patron of the arts—and my hostess for the evening.

"I'm so sorry. I know I must look like a giddy tourist, but we don't have sunsets like this in Dallas."

"Don't apologize," she says. "I pay for that view every month when I write the mortgage check. It damn well better be spectacular."

I laugh, immediately more at ease.

"Hiding out?"

"Excuse me?"

"You're Carl's new assistant, right?" she asks, referring to my boss of three days.

"Nikki Fairchild."

"I remember now. Nikki from Texas." She looks me up and down, and I wonder if she's disappointed that I don't have big hair and cowboy boots. "So who does he want you to charm?"

"Charm?" I repeat, as if I don't know exactly what she means.

She cocks a single brow. "Honey, the man would rather walk on burning coals than come to an art show. He's fishing for investors and you're the bait." She makes a rough noise in the back of her throat. "Don't worry. I won't press you to tell me who. And I don't blame you for hiding out. Carl's brilliant, but he's a bit of a prick."

"It's the brilliant part I signed on for," I say, and she barks out a laugh.

The truth is that she's right about me being the bait. "Wear a cocktail dress," Carl had said. "Something flirty."

Seriously? I mean, *Seriously?*

I should have told him to wear his own damn cocktail dress. But I didn't. Because I want this job. I fought to get this job. Carl's company, C-Squared Technologies, successfully launched three web-based products in the last eighteen months. That track record had caught the industry's eye, and Carl had been hailed as a man to watch.

More important from my perspective, that meant he was a man to learn from, and I'd prepared for the job interview with an intensity bordering on obsession. Landing the position had been a huge coup for me. So what if he wanted me to wear something flirty? It was a small price to pay.

Shit.

"I need to get back to being the bait," I say.

"Oh, hell. Now I've gone and made you feel either guilty or self-conscious. Don't be. Let them get liquored up in there first. You catch more flies with alcohol anyway. Trust me. I know."

She's holding a pack of cigarettes, and now she taps one out, then extends the pack to me. I shake my head. I love the smell of tobacco—it reminds me of my grandfather—but actually inhaling the smoke does nothing for me.

"I'm too old and set in my ways to quit," she says. "But God forbid I smoke in my own damn house. I swear, the mob would burn me in effigy. You're not going to start lecturing me on the dangers of secondhand smoke, are you?"

"No," I promise.

"Then how about a light?"

I hold up the itty-bitty purse. "One lipstick, a credit card, my driver's license, and my phone."

"No condom?"

"I didn't think it was that kind of party," I say dryly.

"I knew I liked you." She glances around the balcony. "What the hell kind of party am I throwing if I don't even have one goddamn candle on one goddamn table? Well, fuck it." She puts the unlit cigarette to her mouth and inhales, her eyes closed and her expression rapturous. I can't help but like her. She wears hardly any makeup, in stark contrast to all the other women here tonight, myself included, and her dress is more of a caftan, the batik pattern as interesting as the woman herself.

She's what my mother would call a brassy broad— loud, large, opinionated, and self-confident. My mother would hate her. I think she's awesome.

She drops the unlit cigarette onto the tile and grinds it with the toe of her shoe. Then she signals to one of the catering staff, a girl dressed all in black and carrying a tray of champagne glasses.

The girl fumbles for a minute with the sliding door that opens onto the balcony, and I imagine those flutes tumbling off, breaking against the hard tile, the scattered shards glittering like a wash of diamonds.

I picture myself bending to snatch up a broken stem. I see the raw edge cutting into the soft flesh at the base of my thumb as I squeeze. I watch myself clutching it tighter, drawing strength from the pain, the way some people might try to extract luck from a rabbit's foot.

The fantasy blurs with memory, jarring me with its potency. It's fast and powerful, and a little disturbing because I haven't needed the pain in a long time, and I don't understand why I'm thinking about it now, when I feel steady and in control.

I am fine, I think. *I am fine, I am fine, I am fine.*

"Take one, honey," Evelyn says easily, holding a flute out to me.

I hesitate, searching her face for signs that my mask has slipped and she's caught a glimpse of my rawness. But her face is clear and genial.

"No, don't you argue," she adds, misinterpreting my hesitation. "I bought a dozen cases and I hate to see good alcohol go to waste. Hell no," she adds when the girl tries to hand her a flute. "I hate the stuff. Get me a vodka. Straight up. Chilled. Four olives. Hurry up, now. Do you want me to dry up like a leaf and float away?"

The girl shakes her head, looking a bit like a twitchy, frightened rabbit. Possibly one that had sacrificed his foot for someone else's good luck.

Evelyn's attention returns to me. "So how do you like LA? What have you seen? Where have you been? Have you bought a map of the stars yet? Dear God, tell me you're not getting sucked into all that tourist bullshit."

"Mostly I've seen miles of freeway and the inside of my apartment."

"Well, that's just sad. Makes me even more glad that Carl dragged your skinny ass all the way out here tonight."

I've put on fifteen welcome pounds since the years when my mother monitored every tiny thing that went in my mouth, and while I'm perfectly happy with my size-eight ass, I wouldn't describe it as skinny. I know Evelyn means it as a compliment, though, and so I smile. "I'm glad he brought me, too. The paintings really are amazing."

"Now don't do that—don't you go sliding into the polite-conversation routine. No, no," she says before I can protest. "I'm sure you mean it. Hell, the paintings are wonderful. But you're getting the flat-eyed look of a girl on her best behavior, and we can't have that. Not when I was getting to know the real you."

"Sorry," I say. "I swear I'm not fading away on you."

Because I genuinely like her, I don't tell her that she's wrong—she hasn't met the real Nikki Fairchild. She's met Social Nikki who, much like Malibu Barbie, comes with a complete set of accessories. In my case, it's not a bikini and a convertible. Instead, I have the *Elizabeth Fairchild Guide for Social Gatherings*.

My mother's big on rules. She claims it's her Southern upbringing. In my weaker moments, I agree. Mostly, I just think she's a controlling bitch. Since the first time she took me for tea at the Mansion at Turtle Creek in Dallas at age three, I have had the rules drilled into my head. How to walk, how to talk, how to dress. What to eat, how much to drink, what kinds of jokes to tell.

I have it all down, every trick, every nuance, and I wear my practiced pageant smile like armor against the world. The result being that I don't think I could truly be myself at a party even if my life depended on it.

This, however, is not something Evelyn needs to know.

"Where exactly are you living?" she asks.

"Studio City. I'm sharing a condo with my best friend from high school."

"Straight down the 101 for work and then back home again. No wonder you've only seen concrete. Didn't anyone tell you that you should have taken an apartment on the Westside?"

"Too pricey to go it alone," I admit, and I can tell that my admission surprises her. When I make the effort —like when I'm Social Nikki—I can't help but look like I come from money. Probably because I do. Come from it, that is. But that doesn't mean I brought it with me.

"How old are you?"

"Twenty-four."

Evelyn nods sagely, as if my age reveals some secret about me. "You'll be wanting a place of your own soon enough. You call me when you do and we'll find you someplace with a view. Not as good as this one, of course, but we can manage something better than a freeway on-ramp."

"It's not that bad, I promise."

"Of course it's not," she says in a tone that says the exact opposite. "As for views," she continues, gesturing toward the now-dark ocean and the sky that's starting to bloom with stars, "you're welcome to come back anytime and share mine."

"I might take you up on that," I admit. "I'd love to bring a decent camera back here and take a shot or two."

"It's an open invitation. I'll provide the wine and you can provide the entertainment. A young woman loose in the city. Will it be a drama? A rom-com? Not a tragedy, I hope. I love a good cry as much as the next woman, but I like you. You need a happy ending."

I tense, but Evelyn doesn't know she's hit a nerve. That's why I moved to LA, after all. New life. New story. New Nikki.

I ramp up the Social Nikki smile and lift my champagne flute. "To happy endings. And to this amazing party. I think I've kept you from it long enough."

"Bullshit," she says. "I'm the one monopolizing you, and we both know it."

We slip back inside, the buzz of alcohol-fueled conversation replacing the soft calm of the ocean.

"The truth is, I'm a terrible hostess. I do what I want, talk to whoever I want, and if my guests feel slighted they can damn well deal with it."

I gape. I can almost hear my mother's cries of horror all the way from Dallas.

"Besides," she continues, "this party isn't supposed to be about me. I put together this little shindig to introduce Blaine and his art to the community. He's the one who should be doing the mingling, not me. I may be fucking him, but I'm not going to baby him."

Evelyn has completely destroyed my image of how a hostess for the not-to-be-missed social event of the weekend is supposed to behave, and I think I'm a little in love with her for that.

"I haven't met Blaine yet. That's him, right?" I point to a tall reed of a man. He is bald, but sports a red goatee. I'm pretty sure it's not his natural color. A small crowd hums around him, like bees drawing nectar from a flower. His outfit is certainly as bright as one.

"That's my little center of attention, all right," Evelyn says. "The man of the hour. Talented, isn't he?" Her hand sweeps out to indicate her massive living room. Every wall is covered with paintings. Except for a few benches, whatever furniture was once in the room has been removed and replaced with easels on which more paintings stand.

I suppose technically they are portraits. The models are nudes, but these aren't like anything you would see in a classical art book. There's something edgy about them. Something provocative and raw. I can tell that they are expertly conceived and carried out, and yet they disturb me, as if they reveal more about the person viewing the portrait than about the painter or the model.

As far as I can tell, I'm the only one with that reaction. Certainly the crowd around Blaine is glowing. I can hear the gushing praise from here.

"I picked a winner with that one," Evelyn says. "But let's see. Who do you want to meet? Rip Carrington and Lyle Tarpin? Those two are guaranteed drama, that's for damn sure, and your roommate will be jealous as hell if you chat them up."

"She will?"

Evelyn's brows arch up. "Rip and Lyle? They've been feuding for weeks." She narrows her eyes at me. "The fiasco about the new season of their sitcom? It's all over the Internet? You really don't know them?"

"Sorry," I say, feeling the need to apologize. "My school schedule was pretty intense. And I'm sure you can imagine what working for Carl is like."

Speaking of …

I glance around, but I don't see my boss anywhere.

"That is one serious gap in your education," Evelyn says. "Culture—and yes, pop culture counts—is just as important as—what did you say you studied?"

"I don't think I mentioned it. But I have a double major in electrical engineering and computer science."

"So you've got brains and beauty. See? That's something else we have in common. Gotta say, though, with an education like that, I don't see why you signed up to be Carl's secretary."

I laugh. "I'm not, I swear. Carl was looking for someone with tech experience to work with him on the business side of things, and I was looking for a job where I could learn the business side. Get my feet wet. I think he was a little hesitant to hire me at first—my skills definitely lean toward tech—but I convinced him I'm a fast learner."

She peers at me. "I smell ambition."

I lift a shoulder in a casual shrug. "It's Los Angeles. Isn't that what this town is all about?"

"Ha! Carl's lucky he's got you. It'll be interesting to

see how long he keeps you. But let's see ... who here would intrigue you ...?"

She casts about the room, finally pointing to a fifty-something man holding court in a corner. "That's Charles Maynard," she says. "I've known Charlie for years. Intimidating as hell until you get to know him. But it's worth it. His clients are either celebrities with name recognition or power brokers with more money than God. Either way, he's got all the best stories."

"He's a lawyer?"

"With Bender, Twain & McGuire. Very prestigious firm."

"I know," I say, happy to show that I'm not entirely ignorant, despite not knowing Rip or Lyle. "One of my closest friends works for the firm. He started here but he's in their New York office now."

"Well, come on, then, Texas. I'll introduce you." We take one step in that direction, but then Evelyn stops me. Maynard has pulled out his phone, and is shouting instructions at someone. I catch a few well-placed curses and eye Evelyn sideways. She looks unconcerned "He's a pussycat at heart. Trust me, I've worked with him before. Back in my agenting days, we put together more celebrity biopic deals for our clients than I can count. And we fought to keep a few tell-alls off the screen, too." She shakes her head, as if reliving those glory days, then pats my arm. "Still, we'll wait 'til he calms down a bit. In the meantime, though ..."

She trails off, and the corners of her mouth turn down in a frown as she scans the room again. "I don't think he's here yet, but—oh! Yes! Now *there's* someone you should meet. And if you want to talk views, the house he's building has one that makes my view look like, well, like yours." She points toward the entrance hall, but all I see are bobbing heads and haute couture. "He hardly ever accepts invitations, but we go way back," she says.

I still can't see who she's talking about, but then the crowd parts and I see the man in profile. Goose bumps rise on my arms, but I'm not cold. In fact, I'm suddenly very, very warm.

He's tall and so handsome that the word is almost an insult. But it's more than that. It's not his looks, it's his *presence*. He commands the room simply by being in it, and I realize that Evelyn and I aren't the only ones looking at him. The entire crowd has noticed his arrival. He must feel the weight of all those eyes, and yet the attention doesn't faze him at all. He smiles at the girl with the champagne, takes a glass, and begins to chat casually with a woman who approaches him, a simpering smile stretched across her face.

"Damn that girl," Evelyn says. "She never did bring me my vodka."

But I barely hear her. "Damien Stark," I say. My voice surprises me. It's little more than breath.

Evelyn's brows rise so high I notice the movement in my peripheral vision. "Well, how about that?" she says knowingly. "Looks like I guessed right."

"You did," I admit. "Mr. Stark is just the man I want to see."

I hope you enjoyed the excerpt! Grab your own copy of Release Me … or any of the books in the series now!

The Original Trilogy
Release Me
Claim Me
Complete Me
And Beyond...
Anchor Me
Lost With Me

More Nikki & Damien Stark

Need your Nikki & Damien fix?

Not only is *Please Me*, a 1001 Dark Nights Nikki & Damien Stark novella releasing August 28, 2018, but there's a brand new *full length* Nikki & Damien book coming in 2018, too!

Lost With Me
Stark Saga, Book 5
Coming Fall 2018

"Sinfully sexy and full of heart. Kenner shines in this second chance, slow burn of a romance. Wicked Grind is the perfect book to kick off your summer."- *K. Bromberg, New York Times bestselling author (on Wicked Grind)*

"J. Kenner never disappoints~her books just get better and better." - *Mom's Guilty Pleasure (on Wicked Grind)*

"I don't think J. Kenner could write a bad story if she tried. ... Wicked Grind is a great beginning to what I'm positive will be a very successful series. ... The line forms here." *iScream Books (On Wicked Grind)*

"Scorching, sweet, and soul-searing, *Anchor Me* is the ultimate love story that stands the test of time and tribulation. THE TRUEST LOVE!" *Bookalicious Babes Blog (on Anchor Me)*

"J. Kenner has brought this couple to life and the character connection that I have to these two holds no bounds and that is testament to J. Kenner's writing ability." *The Romance Cover (on Anchor Me)*

"J. Kenner writes an emotional and personal story line. ... The premise will captivate your imagination; the characters will break your heart; the romance continues to push the envelope." *The Reading Café (on Anchor Me)*

"Kenner may very well have cornered the market on sinfully attractive, dominant antiheroes and the women who swoon for them . . ." *Romantic Times*

"*Wanted* is another J. Kenner masterpiece . . . This was an intriguing look at self-discovery and forbidden love all wrapped into a neat little action-suspense package. There was plenty of sexual tension and eventually action. Evan was hot, hot, hot! Together, they were combustible. But can we expect anything less from J. Kenner?" *Reading Haven*

"*Wanted* by J. Kenner is the whole package! A toe-curling smokin' hot read, full of incredible characters and a brilliant storyline that you won't be able to get enough of. I can't wait for the next book in this series . . . I'm hooked!" *Flirty & Dirty Book Blog*

"J. Kenner's evocative writing thrillingly captures the power of physical attraction, the pull of longing, the universe-altering effect one person can have on another. . . . *Claim Me* has the emotional depth to back up the sex . . . Every scene is infused with both erotic tension, and the tension of wondering what lies beneath Damien's veneer – and how and when it will be revealed." *Heroes and Heartbreakers*

"*Claim Me* by J. Kenner is an erotic, sexy and exciting ride. The story between Damien and Nikki is amazing and written beautifully. The intimate and detailed sex scenes will leave you fanning yourself to cool down. With the writing style of Ms. Kenner you almost feel like you are there in the story riding along the emotional rollercoaster with Damien and Nikki." *Fresh Fiction*

"PERFECT for fans of *Fifty Shades of Grey* and *Bared to You*. *Release Me* is a powerful and erotic romance novel that is sure to make adult romance readers sweat, sigh and swoon." *Reading, Eating & Dreaming Blog*

"I will admit, I am in the 'I loved *Fifty Shades*' camp, but after reading *Release Me*, Mr. Grey only scratches the surface compared to Damien Stark." *Cocktails and Books Blog*

"It is not often when a book is so amazingly well-written that I find it hard to even begin to accurately describe it . . . I recommend this book to everyone who is interested in a passionate love story." *Romancebookworm's Reviews*

"The story is one that will rank up with the *Fifty Shades* and Cross Fire trilogies." *Incubus Publishing Blog*

"The plot is complex, the characters engaging, and J. Kenner's passionate writing brings it all perfectly together." *Harlequin Junkie*

Also by J. Kenner

The Stark Saga Novels:

Only his passion could set her free…

Meet Damien Stark

The Original Trilogy

Release Me

Claim Me

Complete Me

And Beyond…

Anchor Me

Lost With Me

Stark Ever After

(Stark Saga novellas):

Happily ever after is just the beginning.

The passion between Damien & Nikki continues.

Take Me

Have Me

Play My Game

Seduce Me

Unwrap Me

Deepest Kiss

Entice Me

Hold Me

Please Me

The Steele Books / Stark International:

He was the only man who made her feel alive.

Say My Name

On My Knees

Under My Skin

Take My Dare (includes short story Steal My Heart)

Stark International Novellas:

Meet Jamie & Ryan-so hot it sizzles.

Tame Me

Tempt Me

S.I.N. Trilogy:

It was wrong for them to be together…

…but harder to stay apart.

Dirtiest Secret

Hottest Mess

Sweetest Taboo

Stand alone novels:

Most Wanted:

Three powerful, dangerous men.

Three sensual, seductive women.

Wanted

Heated

Ignited

Wicked Nights (Stark World):

Sometimes it feels so damn good to be bad.

Wicked Grind

Wicked Dirty

Wicked Torture

Man of the Month

Who's your man of the month …?

Down On Me

Hold On Tight

Need You Now

Start Me Up

Get It On

In Your Eyes

Turn Me On

Shake It Up

All Night Long

In Too Deep

Light My Fire

Walk The Line

Bar Bites: A Man of the Month Cookbook(by J. Kenner & Suzanne M. Johnson)

Additional Titles

Wild Thing

One Night (A Stark World short story in the Second Chances anthology)

Also by Julie Kenner

The Protector (Superhero) Series:
The Cat's Fancy (prequel)
Aphrodite's Kiss
Aphrodite's Passion
Aphrodite's Secret
Aphrodite's Flame
Aphrodite's Embrace (novella)
Aphrodite's Delight (novella – free download)

Demon Hunting Soccer Mom Series:
Carpe Demon
California Demon
Demons Are Forever
Deja Demon
The Demon You Know (short story)
Demon Ex Machina
Pax Demonica
Day of the Demon

Also by Julie Kenner

About the Author

J. Kenner (aka Julie Kenner) is the *New York Times, USA Today, Publishers Weekly, Wall Street Journal* and #1 International bestselling author of over eighty novels, novellas and short stories in a variety of genres.

JK has been praised by *Publishers Weekly* as an author with a "flair for dialogue and eccentric characterizations" and by *RT Bookclub* for having "cornered the market on sinfully attractive, dominant antiheroes and the women who swoon for them." A five-time finalist for Romance Writers of America's prestigious RITA award, JK took home the first RITA trophy awarded in the category of erotic romance in 2014 for her novel, *Claim Me* (book 2 of her Stark Trilogy).

In her previous career as an attorney, JK worked as a lawyer in Southern California and Texas. She currently lives in Central Texas, with her husband, two daughters, and two rather spastic cats.

More ways to connect:
www.jkenner.com
Text JKenner to 21000 for JK's text alerts.

facebook.com/jkennerbooks

twitter.com/juliekenner